> **In one second he went from relaxed to aroused.**

They were in close quarters, waiting out the rain, when he touched her, and awareness assaulted him with sudden surprise. *Wait a minute*, he told his overeager body. *This is Ellie, my best friend.* "I'd better go," he said, and was amazed by the husk of desire he heard in his voice. "I think the rain may be letting up."

"You think so?" She tilted her head back to listen and his senses were filled with her scent, and her hair—all that wild, fragrant hair curled riotously, sensuously into his awareness. He had to get out of here. Now.

"Ross?" Her voice stopped him. "I just wanted to tell you that no matter what, I still love you. As a friend."

"As a friend," he repeated, as if reminding himself.

He didn't know she was going to hug him until he felt her arms around his waist, until her hair brushed against his nose and mouth, teasing him with its fragrant summer sweetness. And he was positive she didn't know he was going to kiss her until his lips closed over hers and the whole world turned upside down....

Dear Reader,

The forecast this spring is for SHOWERS! Not the gloomy, wet kind that bring May flowers, but the baby, bachelor and wedding kind that bring happiness and true love.

And you're invited to all three! This month Karen Toller Whittenburg hosts a bachelor party—but it's a most unusual one, since the best man happens to be a *woman!*

Join us next month for a raucous bridal shower in Debbi Rawlins's *The Bride To Be...or Not To Be?*

Confetti's falling all spring at American Romance! Don't miss out on any of the fun!

Happy reading!

Sincerely,

Debra Matteucci
Senior Editor & Editorial Coordinator
Harlequin Books
300 East 42nd Street
New York, NY 10017

A Bachelor Falls

KAREN TOLLER WHITTENBURG

Harlequin Books

TORONTO • NEW YORK • LONDON
AMSTERDAM • PARIS • SYDNEY • HAMBURG
STOCKHOLM • ATHENS • TOKYO • MILAN
MADRID • WARSAW • BUDAPEST • AUCKLAND

ISBN 0-373-16727-X

A BACHELOR FALLS

Copyright © 1998 by Karen Toller Whittenburg.

This edition published by arrangement with Harlequin Books S.A.

® and TM are trademarks of the publisher. Trademarks indicated with
® are registered in the United States Patent and Trademark Office, the
Canadian Trade Marks Office and in other countries.

Printed in U.S.A.

Chapter One

"Eliot! Eliot Applegate!"

Stopping short on the corner of Main and Second Streets, Ellie glanced back to see Aunt Ona Mae Hunyacre barreling down the sidewalk toward her.

"Whoa-ho! You're in for it now, Ellie." Overhead, local handyman Henry Boyd grinned down at her from the bucket of a utility truck as he unfurled the Bachelor Daze festival banner he was in the process of stringing across the intersection. "Ona Mae has been having her *dreams* again. Better think of a good excuse quick or you'll be stuck on this street corner until Falls Day."

"Be a pal, Henry," Ellie pleaded. "Rescue me."

Henry swept off his Cardinals baseball cap and ran a hand over his nearly bald head. "Come on, Ellie, who do you think I am? Rapunzel?"

A Bachelor Falls

Ellie stuck her hands into the hip pockets of her overalls. "You're Prince Charming, Henry. Please, lower that bucket and sweep me off my feet."

"Now, don't you go tryin' to sweet-talk me, Miss Eliot. Besides, you know as well as I do, there's no escaping Auntie Om when she's on a tear. She'd just climb up after you and this here bucket ain't big enough for the three of us."

Ellie made a face at him before turning in patient greeting as the town's reigning eccentric bustled up beside her. "Hello, Auntie," she said. "How are you, today?"

"I've been better, Eliot. The ringing in my ears is getting so loud I can hardly hear myself think." The older woman fingered the fifties-style flip of her white hair, checking for stray strands or foreign objects...neither of which was any more likely to appear than the other. "I want to talk to you, Eliot. About a *personal* matter." She frowned at the utility truck and at Henry, who was leaning over the edge of the bucket, eavesdropping shamelessly. "We must talk *privately.*"

"I'd love a chat, Auntie...." Ellie pulled her left hand from her pocket and glanced purposefully at her wrist, although she never wore a watch. "But I've got to get back to the garage.

I just ran downtown to make yesterday's deposit and—''

''You have time for this.'' It was a statement, and when Ona Mae Hunyacre made a *statement,* she brooked no arguments. If she said you had time, then you *had time.*

''Why don't you walk with me?'' Ellie suggested, hoping to corral the dialogue into the ten minutes or so it would take to walk to the auto repair shop. ''We can talk on the way.''

''We'll cross Main Street and sit on that bench in front of Taylor's Shoe Shop,'' Ona Mae stated. And she set out to cross the street then and there, without so much as a glance in either direction, causing Tommie Nell Eubanks to slam on her brakes and tap the horn of her 1976 Plymouth Barracuda. Ellie offered Tommie Nell a glance of apology before she reluctantly followed Auntie Om across the street.

If she had been slightly less demanding or slightly more normal, Ona Mae might not have been so difficult to contend with. She was a dear person, really, and she meant well. Just because she believed in alien abductions and the prophetic nature of her dreams was no cause to snub her. Although, in truth, snubbing her had no effect whatsoever. Ellie—and practically every other resident of Bachelor Falls—had tried everything except downright rudeness to escape

Auntie Om's clutches, only to discover that the best way to handle the problem was with affectionate tolerance. Ona Mae might be two raisins short of being a fruitcake, but she was a part of their community and, as such, she was treated with courtesy and respect.

Ellie did wish she hadn't run into Ona Mae this busy morning, but there was no way to get out of it now. So, with a sigh, she sank onto the old wooden church pew in front of Taylor's Shoe Shop, stretched out her legs and settled in for a rambling discourse on dreams and their interpretations, à la Ona Mae. Overhead, the festival banner flapped in the breeze as Henry arm-wrestled it into submission.

"Sit up straight," Ona Mae instructed, her own back rigid-straight under the beige, polished cotton of her Donna Reed shirtwaist, her skirt tucked protectively over her knees, her snap clasp, cream patina purse propped pertly on her lap. "I don't know how you can dress like the farmer's daughter and expect to find a husband, Eliot. I believe you'd wear those godawful overalls to Sunday morning services if you weren't aware of the ruckus it would raise."

Ellie couldn't keep from smiling. As if a ruckus would have deterred her. "You'll be happy to know OshKosh has come out with a floral print pattern for Sundays and special occasions. Of course, I'm saving my new hot pink pair to wear in Kelly's wedding next month.''

"Hmmph. You're not fooling me, Eliot. I know you're not wearing a pair of tacky pink overalls in the wedding because if there's anyone more stubborn than you, it's Kelly…and she won't let you. You'll wear sea-foam green just like the other maid of honor.''

"Now that Lana's married to Blake, I guess, technically, she'll be the matron of honor and I'll be the maid.''

"Old maid, if you don't change your ways," Ona Mae said with a disapproving sniff. "If God had meant for women to wear pants, he'd have given them hairy legs.''

"Or a dull razor.'' Ellie smiled in the face of the older woman's frown and steered the conversation away from fashion. "I can't decide what I should do with my hair for the wedding.'' She fingered the thick, dark braid looped across her shoulder. "Lana thinks I should wear it loose, but I don't know. I think it would look better pulled through the back of my ball cap in a ponytail. Don't you agree, Auntie?''

Ona Mae's hazel eyes sparkled with humor— well, truthfully, it was just simple aggravation, but Ellie liked to pretend there was more to Aunt Ona Mae Hunyacre than met the eye.

"You young girls have no respect for tradition.

That's the problem, Eliot. However, if Kelly wants to let you dress like an automobile mechanic at her wedding, that's entirely up to her. I'm sure I have nothing to say about it. Right now you and I have more important things to discuss.'' Ona Mae adjusted the position of her purse by a centimeter and lowered her voice, as if she thought the whole town might be listening in…which they probably were. ''Last night I had a dream,'' she whispered dramatically. ''And in my dream, Ross Kilgannon was getting *married.*''

''Really?'' Ellie's interest picked up. ''Was he wearing tacky pink overalls?''

Ona Mae's carefully arched eyebrows arched higher in surprise. ''I must say I expected some concern from you, Ellie. He is still your friend, isn't he?''

Still? Ellie couldn't imagine life without her friendship with Ross Kilgannon. She only wished he were here now to laugh with her over yet another of Ona Mae's ''I had a dream'' forecasts. ''Ross *is* getting married. The day after Falls Day. Remember?''

The stern, white eyebrows reversed direction and drew together in a frown. ''Why wasn't I told about this?''

As if it were a secret, as if the whole town hadn't been talking about Ross's engagement since the *Bachelor Falls Gazette* had printed the official announcement nearly a month ago. "Maybe you forgot," Ellie suggested tactfully.

Impossibly, the older woman's back got straighter. "I hardly think I'd forget something as important as the Kilgannon's only son's betrothal. Obviously the Bostians have interfered again."

Ellie's heart sank as the mysterious Bostians entered the conversation. It was well-known throughout the county—perhaps the whole state of Missouri, possibly the entire world—that Ona Mae Hunyacre believed her fiancé, her beloved Lowell Murtry, had been abducted by aliens over forty years ago. It was well-known for the simple reason that Ona Mae told the sad story to anyone and everyone, whether they wanted to hear it or not. It was not well-known how she had discovered so much about the planet Bost and its inhabitants, the Bostians, but since the purported abduction they had been blamed for miscellaneous misdeeds and mischief, up to, and including, her own forgetfulness.

"Ross's engagement was in the newspaper," Ellie offered as a distraction.

"Not in any issue I've read. No, Eliot, it's perfectly obvious what has happened here. Whatever their devious reasoning, though, I have outwitted the sly little creatures from Bost once again through the power of my dreams.''

At moments like this, it was hard to know what to say, but Ellie gave reality a shot. "So, who was Ross marrying in your dream?"

"Rest assured it wasn't that nitwit blonde from over yonder at Mount Eagle."

"He'll be glad to hear that considering he hasn't dated her since high school."

"And he wasn't marrying that nitwit blonde he brought home from college, either."

Ellie could see her morning evaporating into the list of blondes Ross wasn't marrying. Dearly as she loved him, he had dated a lot of nitwits. "I'll bet you saw him marrying a beautiful, blond accountant from Chicago," Ellie said, hoping to skip straight to the bottom line. "And I'll bet her name is Tori Bledsoe."

"Never heard of her." Ona Mae dismissed Ross's intended bride with an unimpressed sniff. "But I distinctly remember telling Kelly no good would come from the Kilgannon's sending Ross to that backwater university. And to think…he could have been a doctor!"

Ellie looked longingly at the bucket truck and Henry. "Northwestern is hardly a backwater university, Aunt Ona Mae, and Ross *is* a doctor. He's doing his surgical residency in Chicago now."

"He is? *Hmmph.* I'm always the last to know everything. A real doctor, you say. Well, that's good, then. At least, we'll have someone to take over Doc Spivey's practice when he retires."

As if there were a single resident—with the exception of Ona Mae Hunyacre—who thought Ross should hang out his shingle in his hometown. He was Bachelor Falls's pride and joy, and the residents took great delight in discussing his success, even going so far as to claim substantial credit for his having turned out so well. To hear the local wisdom, Ross would have been spoiled rotten by his parents if it hadn't been for the common sense of the townspeople and their influence. To a person, the residents of Bachelor Falls had known Ross was destined for greatness from the moment of his birth. Aunt Ona Mae had prophesied it, due to a particularly vivid dream in which she'd seen Baby Kilgannon conversing with Aristotle, Shakespeare, Picasso, Elvis, and various unknown, but obviously influential, Bostians. So it was decreed from the beginning that nothing was too good for Ross Kilgannon, that no goal was beyond his reach, that he was the town's gift to the world. And it might as well have been a part of the town's charter that when he chose a bride, he would choose someone quite extraordinary.

"Are you *certain* he's going to marry this Chicago girl?" Ona Mae asked suspiciously.

"Ross told me himself," Ellie confirmed. "He called me before he even popped the question and asked me to be the best man in his wedding."

That wrinkled Ona Mae's brow. "You're not wearing overalls to his wedding, are you?"

"No, a tuxedo."

"Pants, again." Aunt Ona Mae made a disapproving click with her tongue. "I certainly hope you aren't planning to be at the bachelor party, too."

Ellie smiled, knowing whatever she said now would be percolating through the Bachelor Falls's gossip hotline within the hour. "Actually, as the best man, it's my job to plan the bachelor party for Ross. I was thinking about making it a shower...you know, something like Lana's baby shower last month. Except I'm not sure if people will know what kind of gifts to give a bachelor."

"I expect a bachelor needs a toaster just as much as a bride does."

"Hmm, maybe." Ellie waved to Jasper as he came out of the bank and she silently pledged to shop exclusively at Jasper's Save-Rite store for the rest of her life if only he'd cross the street and rescue her. He waved back, but walked briskly in the opposite direction...the wily, old rascal. "I don't know. I think a bachelor shower ought to have more imaginative gifts. No appliances. Fun things, but useful, too. Not the towels or linens or kitchen stuff we took to Kelly's shower last week." She pushed to her feet, deciding if no one was going to rescue her, she'd just have to do it herself. As usual. "I really have to get back to the garage, Aunt Ona Mae. It was great talking to you and I'll let you know what I decide about the shower, so you can—"

"Sit down, Eliot." Ona Mae eyed her with ponderous authority. "I'm not through talking to you about Ross Kilgannon. I haven't even told you the dream yet."

Ellie glanced at her wrist again, then at Henry, who waved her back to the bench. He probably hoped she'd keep Ona Mae occupied until he had the banner strung and was safely away from the intersection, saving himself from an earful of Auntie Om's nonsense. "I can only stay five more minutes," Ellie said, as she sank onto the old wooden pew again. "Chip is working today and I don't like to leave him on his own for too long."

"I'll get right to the point then." Ona Mae unsnapped the clasp of her purse, reached in and pulled out a lavender-scented hankie, which she used to dab the tip of her long nose. She then tucked the hankie back inside the purse, and snapped the clasp, leaving an embroidered triangle sticking out of one corner. "In this particular dream, the whole town was gathered in the Methodist Church, which was decorated in purple froo-fras from belfry to basement. Tommie Nell always overdoes the color theme, you know. Thelma Perkins was playing 'Three Blind Mice' on the organ and Melva Whiffington was all set to sing 'I Love You Truly,' although why Ross would let someone who couldn't hit middle C with a coat hanger get up to the microphone at his wedding, I cannot explain."

"It was just a dream, Aunt Ona Mae," Ellie pointed out.

"There's no such thing as *just* a dream, Eliot. Did I or did I not have a dream in which you owned Applegate Auto Repair before your uncle Owen even decided to sell it to you?"

"You did, Auntie," Ellie said with a sigh. It would have been futile to remind Ona Mae that Uncle Owen had told people for years he wanted Ellie to take over his business when he retired. "You did have a dream about the garage."

"Well, then, stop interrupting." She pulled her shoulders back and raised her chin. "If my dream is accurate—and I'm sure it is, because one way or another, my dreams are never wrong—Ross is going to need your help."

"I'll try to talk him out of asking Melva to

sing, if that's what you're getting at, but I don't know if it will do any good.''

''Melva, Schmelva.'' Ona Mae dismissed the details with a jerk of her hand. ''I'm trying to tell you, Eliot, that in my dream Ross wasn't marrying a short little blonde from Chicago.''

''Well, who was he marrying then?''

''A *zebra!*'' Ona Mae said in her best theatrical whisper. ''In my dream, Ross Kilgannon was marrying a *zebra!* And you know what that means...''

''There's a short little blonde from Chicago trapped at the zoo?'' Ellie guessed.

''No.'' Ona Mae cut her eyes in all directions before she whispered excitedly. ''It means trouble,'' came her succinct explanation. ''Trouble in black and white.''

THERE WERE TWO BODIES draped over the front fender of the 1957 Chevrolet when Ellie finally tracked her adolescent apprentice to the back bay of the garage. She identified Chip by the grease-streaked uniform that covered his gangly legs and the worn, dirty Keds that tried courageously to contain his huge—and still growing—sophomore feet. The other body—the one clothed in a good blend of cotton and synthetic tan trousers, the crease of which broke perfectly over the tops of cordovan   loafers   with   a   double layer of shine—was just as familiar. She'd recognize those long legs and tight end no matter what hood they were draped over. All those years of schooling and Ross still didn't have the good sense to change his clothes before investigating the intricacies of a Chevy V-8. She moved closer to the vintage convertible she'd been in the process of restoring ever since she inherited it from Uncle Owen. "Better be careful, she eats would-be mechanics for breakfast."

Thwack! Thwack! Two heads struck the underside of the hood in simultaneous surprise. "Ellie!" Chip frowned and rubbed the back of his head. "Why'd ya always havta sneak up on me like that?"

"If you'd been working up front where I left you, you'd have seen me coming two blocks away." She turned and eyed the other man, who eyed her back with identical interest. "All those years of school and you still can't remember to change your pants before you get close to Hot Rod." She brushed at the line of red primer dust that now streaked his tan slacks midthigh.

"If you'd quit messing around with her bodywork and paint her, I wouldn't have to keep buying new pants." Ross's smile warmed her with its familiarity. The affection in his eyes always made her feel as if the sun were shining just for her.

"Him." She stressed the correction. "The only thing feminine about this Chevy is his owner."

Chip made a scoffing, coughing sound, but she ignored him. Preferring denim to silk and the smell of axle grease to perfume didn't make her less of a woman...at least not in her own eyes. And that, after all, was the only view that mattered. "And you know I can't paint Rod until he tells me what color he wants to be."

"Red," Ross said. "I've told you a thousand times, he wants to be red. Red and white."

"Well, I think he's leaning toward baby blue."

Ross shook his head. "Candy apple red. I'm telling you, Eliot. It would be a crime to paint this automobile any other color. Have I ever led you astray?"

Ellie laughed. "So many times, it's a wonder I'm still speaking to you." Moving forward, she slipped her arm around his waist and hugged him. "I'm glad to see you, Ross. You look..." She stepped back and gave him an appraising once-over. "...great."

He patted his lean stomach with self-satisfaction. "I feel great. Being in love agrees with me."

It certainly appeared to, she thought. From the top of his blond head to the all-American burliness of his brawny shoulders and chest, he looked hale and hardy, healthy and rather alarmingly happy. Ellie felt the first smidgen of unease, but she brushed it aside with the reminder that Ross was twenty-nine years old—old enough to know when he was in love and when he wasn't. "So where is the love of your life?" Ellie asked. "Are you trying to keep her under wraps until the wedding? Because, I warn you, it'll never work. Even as we speak, there's a betting pool going on down at the Save-Rite as to who'll be the first person in town to spot her."

"Oh, man..." Chip's voice trailed into a valley of disappointment. "You mean, I coulda won some dollars? I already seen—saw her. She was right here a few minutes ago. Oh, man..."

Ross clapped the youngster's shoulder. "There's no lotto at the Save-Rite, Chip. That's just Eliot's tacky way of keeping me humble."

Chip looked to Ellie for confirmation and she shrugged. "Sorry, kiddo, no quick cash today—unless you get that bookkeeping caught up for me."

"Ah, Ellie, I hate workin' inside. Couldn't I—?"

"No," she said firmly. "You couldn't. At least, not until the office work is done."

Chip shuffled off, head down, hands thrust into the dingy pockets of his coveralls, defeated.

Ellie smiled. "He doesn't believe me, but there goes the next governor of this great state of Missouri."

"In that case, I'm glad I'm going to be living in Illinois." Ross's gaze followed the dejected teenager as he crossed the dirt and gravel drive of Applegate Auto Repair shop and entered the sunshine yellow clapboard office. "Aren't you shooting a little high for that kid, El? I can see him managing one of my dad's K-Stop stores someday or maybe opening a rival auto shop across the street from you. But governor?"

Ellie cut her gaze to his. "It could happen— and don't you go thinking it can't, either. Chip needs all the positive thoughts he can get. He's having a tough time right now."

"But he's got you on his side, and that means he's going to come through a winner, whether he wants to or not."

"He'll come through a survivor, one way or the other." The office door slammed and Ellie sighed. "At least, if I have anything to say about it." She turned her back on the ordinariness of her own life and smiled at her friend. "So, when did you get into town and when do I get to meet Tori?"

"We flew in this morning. I did the chitchat thing with Mom and Dad, told them what they wanted to hear, then headed for town. I wanted you to be the first person to meet Tori, but you weren't here, so she had to settle for Chip.''

"Obviously he didn't hold her interest for long. Unless..." Ellie glanced suspiciously toward the office. "You guys didn't leave her inside while you came out here, did you?"

"She walked across to Abner's Drugstore to get something. She should be back any minute." Ross arched his eyebrows in self-defense. "I can't believe you'd even ask me that. You know what a courteous guy I am."

"*Mmm-hmm.* I also know how single-minded you get when you start talking about cars, too. She wouldn't be the first date you've left twiddling her thumbs. Remember that time you left Belinda Morgan at the Dairy Queen to go with Shorty Silvers to see a motorcycle? You forgot all about her."

"That was a thousand years ago! And I didn't forget her, I just figured it was so late she'd have gone on home. I didn't know she would sit there waiting for me to come back and walk her home until her parents called mine in the middle of the night and wanted to know where she was." His smile curved with embarrassed amusement. "Sheesh, I can't believe I ever thought I was in love with her. Is she still as, uh, *astute* as she was in junior high?"

"There are those who still refer to her as Bubblehead, if that's what you mean. Not me, personally, of course. You know I never criticized any of the females you chose to grace with your adoration.''

"Like hell, you didn't." He grinned with the ease of long friendship. "I admit I dated a few women who were somewhat IQ-challenged, but you have to admit most of them were pretty bright."

Bright enough to latch onto the most popular, best-looking, finest all-around athlete, most-likely-to-succeed male ever to stroll the halls of Bachelor Falls High School. As if that took much in the way of brains. "Unfortunately an above-average IQ doesn't prevent someone from being a nitwit. And you, Ross, have always been a nit-wit-magnet."

"Was. My foolish-heart days are definitely behind me, now. Wait until you meet Tori," he said with a smile. "She's so...perfect. So sweet and cute and funny and... Well, you'll see for yourself soon enough. You're going to love her as much as I do."

Ellie felt another twinge of unease, but dismissed it as nonsense. Just because she'd heard him say the same things before, just because she recognized that high-beam gleam of infatuation in his eyes, just because it all seemed so completely familiar...well, that didn't mean this time wasn't different. After all, he hadn't come close to getting engaged to any of the other women. "I'm sure I'll be crazy about her, Ross. Although I have to tell you it's going to be hard for me to love anyone who drives a Miata."

He shrugged apologetically. "Her parents gave it to her for graduation and she loves it. What can I say? It was before I met her, before I had a chance to enlighten her, you might say. You'll have to take her under your wing, El. Explain to her the mysteries of the sports car engine."

"Oh, I'm sure she can't wait to have *that* discussion."

"She's interested in everything. You'll see. But she will tell you this car needs to be candy apple red and not blah blah blue."

"If she mentions 'candy apple red,' I'm going to know you coached her on what to say, so you'd better hope she sides with me. Or suggests another paint color altogether."

"She'll say red." He patted the Chevy's fender again, then dusted his hands of the sanded primer. "Hey, Mom told me Lana got married yesterday to some big-shot developer from Texas. And she's already pregnant."

"Yep. He's a really nice guy. I like him a lot." Ellie pulled a rag from her hip pocket and wiped a speck of grease from the chrome valve covers she'd only recently installed on the engine. "The baby's due in August. Kelly's been scrambling around trying to find somebody to modify Lana's bridesmaid's dress. Her wedding's only a month away, you know.''

"All your friends are getting married, El. Any special guy in your future?''

"Sure. I just haven't met him yet. Mabel and Hazel both have nephews they want me to meet, but so far I've been lucky enough to miss their occasional visits.''

"Ah, but Dad said you caught Lana's bouquet at the wedding, so the handwriting is on the wall, my friend. You'll be the next one to get married.''

She offered him a wry look. "You're next, Ross, my man. Not me. And do I have a few things planned for your last week of freedom.''

"I sure hope one of them is a bachelor party. That's probably the only way I'll get to spend any time with the guys this week.''

How naturally he labeled her as one of the guys, Ellie thought, only half-pleased by the inclusion. "Oh, I'll bet neither one of your parents told you what happened at Blake's bachelor party. Belinda was the entertainment.''

"No kidding. What did she do for talent? Twirl her...batons?''

"She used her pom-poms, I believe.''

Ross grinned. "She didn't.''

"Well, in actual fact, all she did was put on her old cheerleader costume and do a couple of high kicks, but you'd have thought from all the gossip that she stripped to the buff."

"Boy, am I sorry I missed that party. Belinda always did look damn good in that short little skirt."

"Not to mention that tight little sweater."

"Did she? I never noticed," he said piously.

She knew better and told him so in a glance. "Well, Belinda's performance has been the hottest gossip item since Tommie Nell got so mad at Mayor Jimmy that she sold the Honda he bought her and traded it for that beat-up old Barracuda."

Ross laughed. A pure and pleasant sound that Ellie loved more than anything. "How did you and I grow up so sane in this crazy town?" he asked.

"Sane? You may have, but I certainly didn't. I'm as crazy as the rest of them. And wait until you hear Auntie Om's latest dream. Trouble for you, Rossy. Trouble in—"

"Ross?" The soft, sexy drawl came from just inside the office's open door.

"Tori." Ross's welcoming smile made even Ellie's heart beat a little faster...and she was completely immune to his myriad charms.

"Come out here, sweetheart, and meet my best friend in the world."

Ellie turned to greet his fiancée, ready to love anyone who loved Ross. She wasn't ready, though, for the woman who stepped from the shadows of the inner office into the noonday sunshine. Tori Bledsoe was petite, busty, blond, cute as a button and looked so much like every other woman Ross had ever loved—Belinda included—that Ellie's heart sank like a stone. Or maybe it was just that Tori was wearing a matching print shorts outfit. A *zebra* print.

Trouble, Ellie thought. *Trouble in black and white.*

Chapter Two

Halfway through the blue-plate special at Hazel's Hash House, Ellie came to the reluctant conclusion that Tori Bledsoe was a nitwit. For the better part of the past hour, Ellie had hoped she was mistaking naïveté and a dewy freshness of spirit for a lack of depth. But midway through Hazel's Run, Boys, Run meat-loaf platter—when Tori smiled beatifically across the table and announced that she and Ross planned to have three children, Kaleb, Kameron and Krystal, all spelled with a *K* to match their last name of Kilgannon—the jig was up.

It wasn't so much the sound of all those *K*s tripping off Tori's tongue that nudged Ellie over the edge, as it was the besotted look on Ross's face as she said it. For him to sit there and trade glorified smiles with a woman who had his entire future mapped out to an alliterative *K* was the final, decisive straw.

Ellie knew that look. She'd seen it many times and she knew in her heart of hearts that Ross was at the peak of infatuation. A pinnacle of adoration that, if past history was a good indicator, would begin a speedy descent sometime very soon. Probably sometime around the second day into his honeymoon. Ellie put down her fork, her appetite disappearing into the abyss of sudden worry.

"...and I'd *sworn* I wasn't going to get into another serious relationship for years and years and then Daddy *insisted* I go with him to what I thought would be just another stuffy old dinner party." At this point in her story of how the two of them had met, Tori reached over and nestled her hand under the protective cover of Ross's, her big blue eyes melting him with one seductive sweep of her lashes. "Well, needless to say, Daddy made sure I was seated next to Ross and that was the end of *that* resolution! The very next morning I told my friend, Chrissy—you'll meet her at the rehearsal dinner Thursday night, Ellie. She's my best friend and Ross just adores her, don't you, sweetie?"

From the look on his face, Ross adored the entire population of the world, including insects. Ellie had always hated this stage of his love affairs. How a man as intelligent, attractive and all-around wonderful as Ross could be reduced to a huge, hulking grin went way past her ability to understand. Certainly she had never been so enamored with a man that she'd needed plastic surgery just to wipe the sappy smile off her face.

"Well, I told Chrissy that very next morning," Tori continued her story. "I said, 'Chrissy, last night I met the man I'm going to marry.'" Impossible as it seemed, the smile brightened. "And two weeks later, he proposed."

Ellie smiled. "No one could ever accuse Ross of being a slow starter when it comes to love."

He frowned meaningfully across the table and, although Ellie privately believed her comment had breezed past Tori without so much as rippling her sails, it seemed Ross thought a clarification was in order. "That didn't come out quite right," she clarified with an easy smile. "What I meant was that Ross has never been the kind of fella who lets the grass grow under him when it comes to romance."

The frown deepened into furrows across his forehead and Ellie raised her eyebrows in a silent *What?* He answered by tightening one corner of his mouth, indicating she should make another attempt. *Damn it,* Ellie thought. If he'd told Tori she was the only woman he'd ever loved, this was going to be a very long week.

"What I really meant to say is that Ross has gobs of experience in following his, uh…heart."

Ross's green-eyed gaze cut sharply to Ellie and then away. "What Ellie is trying so inelegantly to say," he corrected gently for Tori's benefit, "is that I *know* my own heart. *Other* people may spend their energy wondering if they've finally met the right person, but I took one look at you, and *knew* you were the one."

Tori leaned toward him, their lips meeting in a sweetly intimate kiss. Ellie stabbed her meat loaf and wished Ross wasn't always so sure of himself at this stage of a relationship, wished he wasn't always so serenely certain that this love was different from all the rest, wished he wasn't always so all-fired-up confident that this time he was really, truly, deeply in love. Maybe *this* time it was the real thing. Maybe she was being too sensitive, too pessimistic, letting past experience make her uneasy. But then she looked up from the blue-plate special in time to see him give Tori's nose an affectionate tap and Ellie knew Aunt Ona Mae was right. Ross was headed for trouble. Trouble in black and white.

"I've never known a woman mechanic before." Tori's guileless curiosity turned back to Ellie. "Or anyone with a poet's name."

"Eliot's one of a kind," Ross said affectionately.

Ellie shook her head. "Not really. A lot of women are interested in cars and there were several in my auto mechanics classes at Ozark Tech. You'd probably be surprised at how many garages are actually female-owned and operated.''

"I can't imagine working on a car." Tori wrinkled her cute little nose. ''Doesn't grease get under your fingernails?''

"A professional hazard," Ellie admitted, glad that at the moment, her hands were as clean as Tori's, if not as beautifully manicured. "I wear cotton gloves when I can and that helps, but a lot of times I just have to get down and dirty with an engine and depend on my degreaser to save the day.''

"I bet you have to get a manicure every other day." Tori displayed her rose-petal-pink-tipped fingernails on the blue gingham checked tablecloth. "I have my nails done every week now that I'm working. The keypad of my calculator chips the polish something awful." She stopped examining her nail tips and smiled serenely again. "So, what kind of poetry do you write?"

"The worst kind."

"No, really," Tori requested patiently. "Recite one of your poems for me."

"Honestly I'm not much of a poet."

"Oh, Ellie, don't be so modest."

Ellie knew she shouldn't, but the opportunity was there and she just couldn't help herself.

"Roses are red, violets are blue, Ross is a moron when it comes to—"

Ross choked on his iced tea and went into a spasm of coughing.

"Cars," Ellie concluded her poem, as if she had never intended anyone to think she meant to say anything else. "Something go down wrong?" she asked with perfect innocence.

Tori patted his shoulder in concern. "Are you okay, sweetie?"

"Fine," he wheezed. "I'm fine. Ellie's poetry just choked me up, that's all."

"It was a pretty bad poem," Tori agreed, her voice expressing sincere regret and not an inkling of understanding. "You may not have realized it, Ellie, but that last line didn't rhyme."

"She's not a poet, Tori," Ross explained. "She was just named for one."

"Oh." Tori looked enlightened. "Which one?"

"T. S. Eliot," Ellie supplied. "My mother had a crush on him."

"She *knew* T. S. Eliot? Wow."

"She didn't know him," Ross said patiently. "She just liked his poems."

Tori's smile beamed like a flashlight. "Well, aren't you glad she named you after him and not Henry Wadsworth Longfellow? I bet it would be really hard to get a date if your name was Henry.''

"She could be named Edgar Allan Poe and still not have any trouble getting dates. In high school the guys were lined up to take her out.''

"Really?''

There was no need to sound so surprised, Ellie thought, wishing Ross hadn't brought up the subject, knowing she now had to explain. "When our class began turning sixteen, I was the date of choice for any boy with a set of wheels.'' Ellie drew her fork through her mashed potatoes. "My uncle Owen was very generous with his expertise and his garage. It got to be a little embarrassing.''

"For whom?" Ross asked with a laugh. "Every male in town had to live with the knowledge that you knew more about cars than we did.''

"But the two of you never dated, right?'' Tori asked, coming around to the question Ellie felt sure she'd wanted to ask all along. "I mean, you never dated each other, right?''

"No,'' Ross replied.

"No,'' Ellie said just as quickly, exchanging her easy smile for his. "That would have been the end of a beautiful friendship.''

"Not only that, I'd have had to pay somebody else to fix my car every time something went wrong with it.''

"Which would have left you constantly broke." Ellie laughed, just remembering his ancient Toyota. "We had so much fun in that old Land Cruiser."

"Some of the best times of my life were spent in that vehicle."

"I wish you still had her."

"Me, too. I'd take both of you ladies for a spin up to the falls."

Tori stopped slicing the chunks of lettuce in her salad into bite-size pieces. "But you promised your mother and me you'd stay away from the waterfall this week, remember?"

"Don't worry." He stroked his thumb across the back of her hand and gave her another sappy smile. "I'm not about to go jumping in the falls and put the old Bachelor Falls legend to the test."

Tori's smile glowed anew. "That's practically all I've heard since I got into town, Ellie. A complete stranger walked up to me this morning in the drugstore and told me if I wanted to get married Saturday, I'd better hog-tie Ross to a flagpole and throw away the key." Her laughter trilled with high humor. "As if taking a shower in a waterfall could actually stop anyone from getting married. As if it could stop Ross from marrying me."

She sounded pretty confident. Ellie drew a

crosshatch in her potatoes. "Some of the towns-people take the whole Bachelor Daze celebration a little seriously," she said. "But it's all in good fun." She glanced at Ross, who was picking disinterestedly at a tomato buried in his chef salad. "Ross did tell you how the whole thing got started, didn't he?"

"He did," Ross answered with an amiable frown. "I have regaled Tori with the history of our town, including the story of the gold miners who remained unwed by bathing irregularly with homemade soap that turned their skin an unattractive green *and* I've told her the sad tale of Lowell Murtry's kidnapping by the aliens after he had the misfortune of falling in the falls just before he was supposed to marry Ona Mae Hunyacre. I've also instructed her on local etiquette during this week of festivities and she knows the dos and don'ts of Falls Day, namely that I and the other single men in town have to make a run for the falls on Friday and that she has to join the other women in trying to stop us." He stabbed the tomato, sending a tiny splatter of pulp and seeds onto his crisp blue shirt.

"Ross." Tori drew his name into a soft scold as she dipped the corner of her napkin in her untouched glass of water and began dabbing the stain to dilute it. "Look at your shirt. You'll have to change before we meet with the minister this afternoon. Does Bachelor Falls have a good dry cleaners?''

It was just a spot. Hardly even noticeable, but Tori treated it like a blemish of massive proportions, scrubbing vigorously until the stain was thoroughly soaked. And Ross just let her do it. Ellie's appetite gave up the ghost and she laid down her fork. ''So what are your plans for the week, Tori? Did Ross leave you some free time to go over to Branson and see a couple of the shows? There's great shopping, too...if you have the time.''

''My mother has Tori booked every minute between now and Saturday.'' Ross pried the napkin-mop from his fiancée's fingers and gently stopped the stain removal. With a smile, of course, to show he appreciated her efforts, but didn't want her to break a nail or get dishpan hands. ''And in between all the shopping and fittings and family showers, her friends are flying in from Chicago for the wedding.''

''Chrissy is coming on Wednesday.'' Tori took over the recital of coming events. ''The rest of the bridesmaids will be here Thursday and we're going to do lots of girl stuff. You know, we'll have our hair done a couple of times so we can decide how to wear it for the wedding, and there'll be some last-minute alterations on their dresses. Plus they're going to help me gather all the addresses for my thank-you notes. And my family is flying in on Thursday afternoon and I'll want to spend time with them. I've already told Ross not to plan on getting much attention from me until after the wedding.'' She brushed her fingers across his cheek before leaning closer to check the stain again and give it a fleeting disapproval. ''We'll have plenty of time together on our wedding trip, won't we, sweetheart?''

''That's what honeymoons are for.'' Ross turned over a lettuce leaf in his salad bowl and Ellie hoped to heaven he was searching for another tomato. ''Well, Eliot,'' he said absently. ''Looks like your job as best man begins early. Since Tori has as much as told me she doesn't have time for me until our honeymoon, I think it's your duty to keep me out of trouble this week. How are you going to do that?''

''I'll give you a crescent wrench and put you under the hood of my hot rod,'' she supplied easily.

''You won't let him get greasy, will you?'' Tori sounded a little alarmed by the prospect. ''I mean, we'll be having pictures made at the wedding and...''

''It's my duty as best man to deliver your groom to the church on Saturday as stain-free as he is at this minute.'' There, Ellie thought. Worry about that for a while.

"Thanks, Ellie." Tori's smile beamed a thousand unworried watts. "I know I can count on you to take good care of him." She glanced at her watch, then picked up her fork and speared a crouton. "We have plenty of time to finish our lunch. Even if we do have to allow enough time to go back to the house, so you can change shirts." She smiled contentedly at both Ross and Ellie and popped the crouton into her mouth.

Ross looked at the wet circle on his shirt, then at Ellie, and his mouth formed a familiar, stubborn line. *Okay, Ross!* she thought. *Show a little backbone. Show some sense.* Realizing suddenly what she was hoping for, Ellie felt a little ashamed of herself and turned her attention to the slab of meat loaf on her plate.

Hazel, with her wiry sprigs of gray-blond hair and her lean, mean and solid girth, was making the rounds of her diner and she arrived back at their table, as eager to replenish the water in their glasses as she was to discover what they were talking about so she could report it to others in the diner.

"Everybody doin' okay, here?" She wheezed like an old De Soto when she talked and hummed like a freight train when she didn't. "Everybody ready for dessert? I got fresh strawberry pie today. Your favorite, Ross."

"None for us, thanks." Tori leaned forward to

bestow her regret with a flash of dimples. "I have to watch my waistline and Ross doesn't care for sweets." She patted his hand absently as she spoke to Hazel, stroking his long fingers with her shorter ones. "But you probably already know that, since you've been feeding him since he was a little boy."

"I never noticed him skipping *dee*-ssert," Hazel said as she topped off their glasses with water from a red, aluminum pitcher. "Fact of the matter, there was a few years when I flat-out depended on Ross to finish off any *dee*-sserts left over from the day before."

Tori's dimples flashed off, then on again. "Well, he's turned over a new leaf," she said with complete assurance. "He hasn't had a bite of sugar for ages."

"Is tha'so?" Hazel swiped a wet rag across the end of the table, brushing a crumb into her apron pocket. "No wonder he's pale as a nasturtium in a poppy field. Don't you worry none, Miz Bledsoe, I'll get the roses back in his cheeks b'fore Saturdee's weddin'. You just leave it to me." She reached out, picked up Ellie's meatloaf platter, and set it down in front of Ross, pushing his Go, Girls, Go! salad plate toward Ellie. "There now," Hazel said. "Ellie wasn't gonna eat all that, anyway. You polish off that meat loaf and those mashed potatoes while I go

back and get you a hunk of that strawberry pie."
And she bustled off to the kitchen, a woman with
a mission.

Ross exchanged an amused glance with Ellie.
"Guess you're through eating, Eliot."

"Guess so," Ellie said good-naturedly. "I
didn't really want any more, anyway."

"You didn't eat much." He glanced suspiciously from the barely touched meat loaf to her.
"Is there something wrong with this? Hazel
hasn't lost her magic touch, has she?"

"Those are fighting words around here, Ross.
You know that. The only thing that can compete
with Hazel's meat loaf is Mabel's chicken-fried
steak. Mabel's Diner is across the street," Ellie
added for Tori's benefit. "There's been a not-so-
friendly rivalry going on between the two café
owners as long as I can recall."

Ross laughed. "Remember the year Mabel
started the Festival Feasts?"

"Don't say that too loudly," Ellie whispered
with a corresponding grin. "I don't think this
town could survive another recipe war."

Tori looked from Ross to Ellie expectantly,
wearing the questioning expression of someone
who doesn't get the joke.

"A few years ago," Ellie explained, "Mabel
came up with the idea of creating a whole new
menu for the Bachelor Daze celebration. She told

everyone she was having trouble sleeping, so she spent her nights thinking up new recipes and printing up new menus, which she posted on the diner window the next morning. Not to be outdone, Hazel also dreamed up some new dishes and posted a new menu on her window. *She* claims it was pure coincidence that the two diners had different menus, but the same, exact food. Mabel was furious and she went underground, blacking her windows and creating her masterpieces in the dark. But the next day, when Hazel's menu went up in the window, it was all but identical to Mabel's.''

Tori's smiled ranged from Ross to Ellie and back again. ''Was there a *spy* in Mabel's kitchen?''

''Aunt Ona Mae Hunyacre was sure it was the Bostians trying to get in on the festival in their own annoying and alien way.'' Ross's eyes crinkled with humor and Ellie knew he was remembering, as she was, the night they'd snuck out at midnight to do a little adolescent sleuthing. They'd seen Ona Mae out, too, but although they waited until nearly dawn, they never saw her go into Mabel's house or come out of Hazel's. But they'd always figured she had to be somehow responsible for stirring up the great recipe war. ''There are lots of theories around town, the most popular being that Hazel and Mabel cooked up the whole scheme to drum up business." Ross scooped a bite of meat loaf onto his fork with undisguised relish. "Ellie and I have always given that theory short shrift, though, because we don't believe either Hazel or Mabel could keep a secret long enough for it to *become* a theory. That's why we're particularly partial to the alien-conspiracy idea."

"Oh, Ross, you're such a tease." Tori said, beaming her smile on him and showering Ellie with its brightness by default. "Has he always been such a cutup, Ellie?"

"Always," Ellie agreed, although *cutup* was not the word she would have chosen in reference to Ross. "In school, he was always *cutting up,* but then, he was always teacher's pet, too."

"Oh, I was not." Ross said before thrusting the forkful of meat loaf into his mouth and chewing enthusiastically.

"Was he really?" Tori asked, clapping her hands in delight. But her smile faded when she saw the second bite of meat loaf headed for Ross's mouth. "I didn't know you ate beef," she said, making the entrée sound as appealing as roadkill stew.

Ross paused with the tines of his fork hovering a bare quarter inch from his mouth, the savory meat loaf, which was one of Hazel's jealously guarded secret recipes, tantalizingly close to his tongue. He looked at Ellie and, just for an instant, she thought she saw the first flash of sense returning, but then he put down his fork and pushed the plate back across the table. "I've been trying to eat healthier the past few months," he said by way of explanation.

Tori's smile bounced back. "This residency has enough stress built in without adding an artery-clogging diet on top of it. Daddy's a real stickler for keeping his residents healthy and happy."

Ross pulled the salad platter away from Ellie and picked up his fork again with a definite lack of enthusiasm. "Tori's a strict vegetarian. She's incredibly disciplined about it."

"He makes me sound like a saint." Tori's pleasure oozed out in a delighted, little laugh. "But the truth is, I just can't bring myself to pollute my body with animal fat and the chemical additives put into feed stock these days. Daddy says only one out of every ten thousand Americans has clear, uncluttered veins. Isn't that just unbelievable?"

"Unbelievable," Ellie replied, looking around the diner, hoping to see one undeniably healthy person to refute the evils of animal fat ingestion. But the people in Hazel's Hash House hadn't come there to eat vegetables and fruit. On the other hand, they all—from Mayor Jimmy and

Tommie Nell to three-year-old Nicky Newman and his mom—looked robust and healthy. Then again, on the *other* hand, Tori was no slouch in the looking-healthy department, either. Ellie felt a little sickly just sitting across the table from her.

"Here we go." Hazel set a plate with a good fourth of a strawberry pie on it in front of Ross. "Now, I don't want to find so much as a crumb left on that plate next time I stop by this table, you hear me, Ross Kilgannon?" The salad plate was gone in a flash, combining what Ellie thought was some sleight of hand on Ross's part as well as Hazel's.

"She's kind of *pushy,* isn't she?" Tori stared at Hazel's retreating rear end, apparently oblivious to Ross's part in the plate exchange and the hungry, lustful expression in her beloved's eyes when he looked at that strawberry pie. Her smile returned to him like a blessing. "I can wrap that in a napkin and carry it out in my purse," she offered, blithely indifferent to the casual, but definitely defensive, way he cupped his hands around the pie plate. "I'll throw it away and she'll never know you didn't eat every bite. I mean, you *don't* want to eat all that *sugar,* do you?"

He did. Ellie could read his thoughts like a book at that moment, and he wanted that pie. He wanted every last crumb of it. She settled back to see how true love handled a piece of strawberry pie.

"It would really hurt her feelings, Tori," Ross began his campaign. "I have to eat at least a bite of it. I'm sure she's watching. Hazel's just that way."

With one sweeping glance, Tori ascertained that Hazel not only wasn't watching, she had her back turned. "Give me that pie," she whispered, reaching for the plate. "I'll have it out of sight before she turns around."

He scooted the plate a short distance away from her fingers. "But she'll think I gobbled it down in two bites."

"Oh." Tori frowned. "Okay, we'll wait a few more minutes, then I'll grab it."

Gobbling, apparently, would be worse than consuming all that sugar, Ellie decided, smiling cheerfully at Ross's dilemma. "If you're not going to eat it, hand it over," she said forcefully. "Hazel's pies are too wonderful to waste."

Tori seemed startled that anyone would make such an offer. "Well, if you're sure you *want* it," she said.

You'll get this over my dead body, was the silent message in Ross's murderous frown.

Delighted as much by the interplay as by the anticipated taste, Ellie leisurely pulled the plate away from Ross, fork and all. "Mmm," she said. "This looks yummy."

"It would be better for you if you'd wash that jelly stuff off of the berries." Tori folded the napkin and tucked it back inside her roomy, black patina purse. "But I guess if you're accustomed to eating sweets, you like it that way."

She didn't have to make it sound as though Ellie consumed a pound of sugar at each of twenty meals a day. It wasn't as if Ellie outweighed Tori by more than ten pounds, if that much. It was just that her overalls disguised her shape a little better than Tori's zebra-striped shorts disguised hers. And the pie was worth its weight in gold. It was, as Hazel's pies always were, utterly, completely delicious.

Ross watched her chew with something very near jealousy. "Good?" he asked and Ellie nodded, feeling a little guilty for eating his pie. But not guilty enough to stop eating it. It was his own fault, really. If he was truly in love with Tori, he should have been able to tell her he liked pie. Did he think he could keep eating nothing but vegetables for the rest of his life?

The rest of his life. The strawberries seemed suddenly tart and not nearly as sweet. Ross was going to marry Tori and give up pie for the rest of his life. And there wasn't a damn thing Ellie could do to stop it. She'd tried to burst the bubble of infatuation in the past and been rewarded with a few choice words which should never be exchanged between friends...even if one of them was a knucklehead who apologized afterward, admitting he hadn't been thinking straight, and asking *her* how he could have ever imagined he was in love with such a nitwit.

But through the years of watching Ross fall in and out of love, Ellie had picked up a couple of absolute rules for their friendship. Hands off. Mouth shut. Agree with anything he said about the apple of his eye until he came to his senses and asked her why she hadn't told him he was merely in the throes of yet another infatuation. Ellie knew the routine. Except this time when Ross came to his senses, he'd be married. Forever. And he'd never get to taste another bite of Hazel's strawberry pie.

"We'd better get going." Tori took a last, long sip of her drink, then looked at Ross expectantly. "We don't want to keep Reverend Minks waiting." Her gaze turned to Ellie. "Ross and I have a phobia about being late. Just drives us crazy to be running behind schedule. He simply refuses to be hurried."

Ross avoided Ellie's questioning gaze—probably because he knew what she was thinking—and slid from the booth, allowing Tori to slide out after him. "Why don't you go on out to the car while I take care of the bill?'' he suggested. ''Hazel will want to talk and if you're already outside, I can honestly tell her that I can't keep you waiting while we chat.''

Tori nodded and went up on tiptoe to kiss his chin. ''You think of everything,'' she said in a very nitwit-y tone of voice. ''Bye, Ellie. I'm so glad we've had some time to get acquainted. I hope I'll see you again before the rehearsal dinner Thursday night. Maybe you'd like to go with me and my bridesmaids for a manicure later in the week.''

''That sounds lovely,'' Ellie said without so much as a blink at the lie. ''I'll look forward to it.''

''Bye.'' Tori waved like Miss America to Hazel and anyone else who happened to be watching her exit. Which happened to be everyone in the diner. ''Thank you. Bye.''

Ross watched her until the bell over the front door chimed the news of her exit. Then he plopped onto the bench seat and grabbed the pie plate right out from under Ellie's fork. ''Give me that,'' he said. ''I'm in a hurry.'' Then he ate all that remained of the strawberry pie.

Chapter Three

Ellie knew even before she opened her door that Ross would be on the other side and still, she was somehow surprised to find him there.

"Hi," he said, his hands shoved casually into the pockets of a pair of tight, faded blue jeans. "Is it too late to drop by? You weren't already in bed, were you?"

"It's only nine o'clock, Ross. Even here in backward Bachelor Falls, we get to stay up until ten."

"But only on weekends, if I remember correctly."

"True, but as the Bachelor Daze festival runs through Saturday, Mayor Jimmy has decreed that the streets don't get rolled up until eleven. And Friday night, for the Falls Day Street Dance, everyone gets to stay up an extra hour to midnight in honor of the newly showered and newly *un*-showered bachelors." She stepped back and held the door open for him. As if he needed an invitation. "So, Mr. Kilgannon, this is your lucky week."

"I knew there was a good reason I came home just now." Ross walked past her and immediately looked as familiar and comfortable in her front room as the slip-covered furniture.

She closed the door behind him and leaned back against it. "I thought maybe you chose this week so you could accidentally shower in the falls and escape your impending matrimony."

He frowned amiably. "You've been in this town too long, Eliot. You're beginning to sound like the natives."

"I am a native, Ross. Just like you. And you know I don't believe that getting dunked in our famous falls, whether by accident or design, is going to keep anyone from getting married, no matter how many stories folks around here like to tell to the contrary. I was just teasing you a little, trying to see if you were getting cold feet."

"Cold feet?" One of his eyebrows angled sharply, defensively. "Why would you say that?"

She shrugged. "No particular reason. I was only joking."

"Well, for your information, I'm not getting cold feet. I mean, why would I? Tori's great. She's perfect. Everyone who meets her falls in love with her.'' He narrowed his green eyes at Ellie's composed and noncommittal expression. ''And you can wipe that expression right off your face, Eliot. I know what you're thinking, but Tori is different. I'm crazy about her and I'm going to marry her.''

If Ellie had needed further proof that this was infatuation and not the real thing, the defensive note in his voice offered sufficient grounds for suspicion and the tense set of his shoulders weighed in as pretty strong evidence, too. But she was keeping her opinions to herself. At least she would keep her mouth shut on this, his first night back in town and possibly the only opportunity she might get to spend time alone with him. ''I wasn't going to say anything negative, Ross. Tori is wonderful. I like her very much and I can see that you're crazy about her. I'm happy for you. I really am.''

He nodded, his tension easing, as if he'd expected an argument and was relieved when it didn't materialize. ''I just had to get out for a while,'' he explained, even though she hadn't asked. ''A guy can only talk so much about weddings before going stir-crazy, you know.'' He moved through the front room and into the kitchen, where he opened the refrigerator door and stood in the soft, artificial glow while he studied the contents of the shelves.

"There's a leftover salad in the crisper." Ellie moved to the kitchen doorway, crossed her arms over her terry-cloth robe, and tried to absorb some of the energy Ross always seemed to bring with him wherever he went. After Saturday she doubted he would have much occasion to walk into her house again as if he belonged there. After Saturday she doubted she'd have many more opportunities to just stand and watch him check out the food in her fridge. "There may even be some carrots in a bag, already peeled and ready to eat."

He didn't acknowledge her offer of healthy choices, just moved things around, pulled out the milk carton and set it on the counter, his expression turning hopeful. "What have you got to go with this?" he asked. "Your mom's chocolate chip cookies, maybe?"

"No. Sorry. Mom's in California visiting my aunt Shirl, and I've been too busy keeping up with the garage and the garden to do any baking. She had this trip planned for ages and, unfortunately, she's going to miss the wedding Saturday, but she said to give you and Tori a big kiss and her best wishes."

Ross looked wistfully at the milk carton, then set it back on the shelf and closed the refrigerator door. "Want to go over to Ernie's and shoot some pool?"

"With you?"

"Of course with me. I wasn't suggesting you should go by yourself and leave me here with your empty refrigerator."

He certainly sounded testy this evening. "Do you want something to eat?" she asked. "There may be some ice cream in the freezer."

"Thanks, but I'm not really hungry. Just a little on edge, I guess."

A lot on edge, Ellie thought, but knew better than to say. "You seemed fine this afternoon when we left Hazel's."

"I was fine. I *am* fine. I just wanted to put on an old pair of jeans and a T-shirt and get out of my parents' house for a while. Do you have a problem with that?"

"No, of course not. I'm just a little surprised is all."

"I don't know why you would be. I always show up at your house sooner or later. And it's not like I left Tori to twiddle her thumbs, you know. She and my mother were counting place settings when I left. I think we're up to some ungodly number like seventeen or twenty-three, or something distressingly uneven."

Ellie bit back a smile at the long-suffering expression on his face. "Place settings, huh?"

"Look, don't give me a hard time about this tonight. All I want is a little companionship and a conversation that doesn't revolve around dresses, flowers, rehearsal dinners, bridesmaids, wedding ceremonies or place settings.''

"Hmm. I'd hoped we could discuss which pocket I should keep Tori's ring in during the ceremony, but if you're not in the mood..." She loved the flash of exasperation in his eyes, knowing it had nothing to do with her. "And I would like to know what color boutonniere all of us groomsmen will be wearing, but I can wait to find that out. I don't have to know this instant."

"The boutonnieres are going to be a single, summer-watermelon-pink rosebud tied with spring-showers-green ribbon and a sprig of albino parsley." He rubbed the back of his neck as if it pained him, then continued in a dismal tone of voice. "Those are *our* colors, Tori tells me. The pink and the green. I just made that up about the parsley."

She laughed. "I sort of figured that."

"Did you? Tori didn't think it was very funny."

"Oh."

"Oh?" he repeated on a frustrated sigh. "What do you mean, *'Oh?'*"

Ellie straightened and pushed away from the door frame. "I *said,* 'Oh,' and I *meant,* 'Oh.' And don't you go thinking I'll let you beat me at billiards just because you're in a bad mood, either. While you've been gone, I've been getting in a lot of practice and I *will* whip your socks off.''

Humor made a leisurely return to his eyes. ''Well, I suppose you can try.''

''No trying to it,'' she assured him. ''The first time you line up a shot, I'll start humming *Lohengrin*.'' She demonstrated the first few notes of the wedding march in a threatening hum. ''All's fair in love, war and billiards, you know.''

''Put your money where your mouth is, Eliot. Let's go.''

''Give me fifteen minutes to change clothes and you're on.''

''You look great as you are. Let's go.''

Ellie shook her head, wishing that just once Ross would pay some slight attention to what she was or wasn't wearing. ''I'm changing,'' she said unequivocally. ''No matter how much you try to turn my head with your pretty compliments, I am not wearing my bathrobe to Ernie's. It'll only take a few minutes. Make yourself comfortable,'' she added, as if he wasn't already as much at home in her house as she was.

He opened the freezer door. ''Did you say you have some ice cream?''

''Yellow plastic bowl. Next to the frozen pound cake.''

Ross's *mmm-mm* of anticipated pleasure followed her all the way down the hall and until she closed her bedroom door.

THE WILD MOUSE BAR AND GRILL was as sleazy as it was possible to be in conservative Bachelor Falls. It was more bar than grill, but Ernie Potts, the proprietor, didn't want anyone—particularly Hazel or Mabel—accusing him of running a beer joint, so the menu featured a single entrée. A cheese-and-onion sandwich, which Ernie grilled on a hot plate upon request. And he got a lot of requests.

The place always smelled of onions and beer and echoed with lots of laughter and some pretty tall tales. When it wasn't out of order, the juke-box played Ernie's favorite mix of music—a little country, a little rock and roll and a lot of western swing. Ernie had asthma and consequently, there was no smoking allowed on the premises. He diligently checked IDs—as if everyone in town didn't know the age and birth date of everyone else—and absolutely no one under twenty-one was admitted for any reason. Over the years, getting into The Wild Mouse had become a rite of passage eagerly awaited or fondly remembered by practically everyone who grew up in Bachelor Falls.

Ellie spent much of the four-block walk to the bar telling Ross why none of their old gang was likely to be shooting pool at Ernie's on a Monday night. But as if they expected one of their own to return, three longtime friends were chalking pool cues when Ross and Ellie walked in.

"Ross!" Shorty Silvers, a very tall, very lanky young man, hollered across the bar. "Hey, buddy, we were just talking about you. Hey, Ellie."

"Hey, Shorty." She approached the table, nodding to each of the men in turn, using the Ozark greeting of "hey" in place of "hi." "Hey, Travis. Hey, Bobby Joe."

"Hey, Ellie." They greeted her in return, their smiles going straight to her companion.

Bobby Joe slapped his arm around Ross's back and escorted him to the billiard table in play. "It's about time you returned to your roots, son. Rack 'em, Travis. I'm gonna beat the pants off our illustrious doctor, here."

"You'll have to get in line," Ross said with a laugh. "Ellie's already called dibs on my socks."

"Ellie always did think like a girl." Bobby Joe shook his head and gave her a haven't-we-taught-you-better look. "You've got to make the prize interesting, or else what's the point?"

"Ernie!" Travis yelled at the bartender. "Bring Ross a beer and put it on my tab."

Ernie came around the end of the bar before Travis had finished his order. "Welcome home," he said, giving Ross's hand a firm shake. "You want a beer? A sandwich? You name it, boy, and it's yours. On the house."

"Hey, Ernie," Shorty complained. "How come you never say that to the rest of us? Aren't we your best customers?"

"Yeah," Travis joined in good-naturedly. "Ross deserted you for the big city."

"He left home to make something of himself." Ernie dismissed the complaints as he wiped down the counter. "Wasn't content to hang around a pool hall like the rest of you yahoos."

"Now, Ernie." Travis straddled a nearby chair. "Some of us had to stay in Bachelor Falls and be your customers. Otherwise Ross wouldn't have a place to play pool when he does decide to come home."

"Yeah, Ernie." Bobby Joe lent moral support. "Anybody would think going to the community college, like all of us did except Ross, wasn't good enough."

Ernie tucked the bar rag in his apron pocket, unimpressed by the argument. "Ain't his fault the rest of you didn't apply to med school, now, is it?"

Ross chose a cue from the rack on the wall and handled it with loving regard. "You give me too much credit, Ernie. If Ellie hadn't broken her ankle the summer we were fifteen and decided one of us ought to become a doctor, I probably would have stayed right here in Bachelor Falls and become the local pool hustler. And I'd have been a damn good one, too. Certainly better than any one of these guys, that's for sure.''

"Yeah, yeah." Ellie racked the balls into a triangle of solids and stripes and stepped back from the table. ''You've always been a big talker, Kilgannon. Now, show us what you learned in the big city. Break.''

The other men grinned in approval. "You tell him, Ellie."

He eyed her with a smile of practiced tolerance. "All right," he said magnanimously. "I just hope maturity has taught you to be a good loser because you are not getting a pair of my socks tonight." And with that, he sighted the cue ball and sent it spinning, breaking the triangle and neatly pocketing the number-ten ball in the corner pocket.

''Beginner's luck,'' Ellie muttered and thought how very much she'd missed him. She felt so lucky to be here with Ross now, to be watching the precise way he sized up a shot, the lean intensity of his body as he moved around the table, the satisfied set of his jaw when the ball spun unerringly into the called pocket. She liked everything about him, even the way he looked in his old jeans, and she hoped with all her heart that Tori understood and appreciated the man she was about to marry.

"You may as well start saying your prayers, Eliot." Ross pointed the cue stick at the eight ball and then to the side pocket. "Because I am about to own your socks."

"I'm not wearing any, but I'll give you a place setting of china as a trophy," Ellie said.

He missed the shot and the cue ball slid into the pocket. Ellie blew imaginary smoke from the end of her cue stick, winning without ever having taken a shot. "I love it when that happens. Hand over those socks, my friend."

"I demand a rematch," Ross said pleasantly. "On the grounds that you took advantage of my prenuptial state of mind."

"That's right," Travis said. "He's a doomed man and it's flat-out cheating to remind him of it just before a shot."

Bobby Joe laughed. "He's doomed, all right. Five more days, Ross, until those church bells toll for you."

"The old ball and chain. I made a narrow escape myself just last year." Shorty tipped his beer bottle to his lips in commiseration. "Take my advice and get the hell out to the falls before it's too late."

"I already suggested that," Ellie said. "And he assured me he *wants* to get married."

Travis put a hand on Ross's forehead. "He's feverish. Talking out of his head."

"Marriage isn't so bad." Bobby Joe patted Ross's shoulder sympathetically. "Not for the first few days, anyway."

"Yeah, but after that..." Travis turned his thumbs down and shook his head sadly. "Listen to us, Ross. We know whereof we speak, don't we, Bobby Joe?"

Ellie cleared her throat loudly and used her pool cue to tap Travis on the shoulder. "Tami is the best thing that ever happened to you, Trav, and you know it. And Bobby Joe, don't try to con us into thinking you're not the one who *begged* Carla to marry you. Ross and I were there. We stopped you from serenading her with that stupid song you wrote, remember? If she'd heard you sing that, it's for sure you'd still be single."

"Well, thanks a lot. You could have saved me and you didn't." Bobby Joe tried to act offended, but wound up with a wry smile. He and Travis were both very happily married, and for all their bravado and macho denials, they didn't fool anyone. "Did you hear that, Travis? If it hadn't been for Ross and Ellie, I'd be a free man today."

Ross laughed, recalling a few of the great

times he'd spent with these people. It always seemed so effortless and easy to fall back into the comfortable routines of good friends and familiar surroundings. He'd needed this, he realized. A little relaxation with people who accepted him for himself, who didn't ask him a lot of questions, who didn't expect him to be strong or smart or smitten with the glaze on a china plate. His gaze swept the rustic interior of The Wild Mouse, and he smiled. It was good to come home, no matter what Thomas Wolfe had written on the subject.

"I'm looking forward to Saturday," he said, watching as Ellie broke the racked balls for their rematch. "There comes a time for a man to settle down with the right woman…and Tori's right for me."

"Did you say *ripe?*" Travis grinned wickedly. "Rumor has it, she's blond, gorgeous and has great big—"

"Blue eyes," Ellie supplied succinctly, overriding Travis's baser statement and reminding not-so-gently that there was a limit to what they could and couldn't say in her presence. Ross had always admired her ability to be "one of the guys" without giving up her femininity. Ellie wasn't a prude by any means, but she expected respect and she never let any of her male friends forget it.

"I was gonna say that," Travis protested, including the other men with a broad wink. "I was gonna say I heard Ross's woman had great big blue eyes."

Ellie straightened and turned to look at him, her cue stick in hand. "How long before Tami gets back from visiting her cousin in St. Louis?"

"She just left this evening," Travis said, looking puzzled. "How'd you know she was gone?"

"Lucky guess." Ellie made another difficult shot and Ross decided she had been practicing. Maybe she hung out here at Ernie's with these guys more than he'd thought. "Or maybe, Travis," she continued, "it's because you only act like an adolescent when she's out of town. Ross's *woman*." She shook her head. "I'd like to hear you say that in front of Tami."

"Ellie's got you dead to rights, man." Bobby Joe leaned back against the bar, nodding agreement. "Carla would tie my pecker in a knot if she ever heard me say somethin' like that. I bet Tami wouldn't like bein' called Travis's *woman* any better."

"She wouldn't mind it so much," Travis said, but his tone lacked true conviction.

"That's one of the great things about Tori," Ross said, smiling at the thought. "She's not so sensitive about little slips of the tongue like that." Ellie and her pool cue turned slowly in his direction and he realized how that must have sounded. ''Not that I'd ever refer to her as my *woman,* of course. And I didn't mean she was insensitive to women's issues.''

Ellie didn't say a word, just looked at him, but he knew her too well and could read her thoughts almost verbatim. *Tori,* she was thinking, *is a nit-wit.* Tori wasn't a nitwit, but Ross figured the best defense at the moment was not to say so out loud.

Ellie circled the table, eyeing the best shot and lowering her cue. ''Six ball in the corner.'' She indicated the pocket, then bent to attempt what Ross considered a completely impossible shot. She made it…even though he was rooting against her.

''You're all invited to the wedding,'' Ross said, hoping to distract her enough so she'd miss a shot. ''It's at the Methodist Church. I hope you'll all be there.''

''You going, Ellie?'' Shorty asked, stroking his chin. ''I could come by and pick you up, if you want. We could go together.''

''She's my best man,'' Ross said quickly. ''We'll have to be there early. Together.''

''Thanks, but it looks like I'm going to have my hands full taking care of our eager groom Saturday.'' Ellie gave Shorty what Ross considered to be one of her all-time best smiles. She had the kind of wide, openmouthed smile that could knock men for a loop, and Ross didn't much like her encouraging a guy who had had a crush on her since second grade. It wasn't that Shorty wasn't a nice guy. He was. But Ellie wasn't ever going to have reciprocating feelings for him and it wasn't fair of her to bestow that kind of smile just because she had to turn down his offer of a ride. "But after the ceremony," she continued, still smiling. "Maybe we could—"

"Dance," Ross supplied smoothly, wondering if he could accidentally bump the table, ruin her next shot and wipe that smile off her full lips. "There's a reception at my parents' house and, of course, you're all invited to that, too. There'll be lots of champagne and music, so Ellie can save you a dance, Shorty. If she wants to, that is."

He was aware of the slightest frown on Ellie's brow, but he didn't acknowledge that he'd been a bit high-handed in arranging her after-the-wedding schedule. Besides, she'd want to stay at the reception. She'd want to have at least one dance with the groom. Maybe more. They were still going to be friends, even after he was married. And he wasn't going to stand by and watch her start dating someone so not-her-type as Shorty Silvers. Ross checked the slight tightening of her mouth and amended his silent avowal. Unless she really wanted to.

"Save me a dance, too, Ellie." Bobby Joe stepped around the end of the bar and motioned to Ernie for another beer. "I couldn't miss this wingding, even if I wanted to, Ross. Carla's already bought a new dress and she and Tami have had their heads together for a month, ever since the announcement came out in the paper, trying to come up with the perfect wedding gift."

"Let's tell them to buy him a new billiard cue," Travis suggested. "Ross needs some practice."

"You gotta get something for their house, knucklehead." Shorty set his beer aside and rechalked his cue stick, undoubtedly anticipating Ross's imminent defeat.

"Yeah," Bobby Joe said without enthusiasm. "That's another thing about getting married, Ross. All the stuff you'd like to have, like a pool cue or a set of golf clubs or a fishing rod, makes the women laugh. Like they think you're being really funny by saying it. But the stuff they want, like towels and dishes, well, that's the stuff people give you tons of at your wedding showers. It's like your opinion doesn't matter even before you get hitched."

"The idea is to give something a *couple* can use," Ellie said pointedly. "And men do occasionally have a use for a towel and even for a place setting of china.''

''I'd have let Carla use my cue stick,'' Bobby Joe stated generously.

''Yeah.'' Travis got into the spirit. ''And Tami likes to fish. Someone could have given us matching fishin' poles.''

Ellie lined up another shot and sank it, leaving Ross two balls away from a second defeat. ''The idea is to furnish a home for the newlyweds,'' she said.

''But men aren't particular about furnishings, you see.'' Travis picked up the complaint and took it further. ''A man doesn't care what color the towel is when he steps out of the shower, and when he's hungry, he sure as hell doesn't care if his dishes are made out of paper or china. Dishes are wasted on men, anyway.''

''Ditto on silverware,'' Bobby Joe said, eyeing the eight ball which was right in line with the corner pocket and directly in the way of a clear shot. ''Watch out for the eight,'' he advised Ellie before continuing his *he-man* theorizing. ''A man can get by with just a fork. Remember all those times we camped out at the falls and didn't even bother to take plates or anything? In the final analysis, a can opener's the only thing a real man needs.''

''You're abso-damn-lutely right, Bobby Joe.''

Feeling as macho as possible while having his socks whipped off, Ross settled back on a bar stool to watch Ellie sweep the final shot. "I'd forgotten just how far we've gotten away from a man's basic needs."

"Only a can opener away from the caveman," Ellie observed dryly, setting her cue stick aside and taking the bar stool next to his. "How can you leave this cradle of civilization behind, Ross? You're going to marry a beautiful woman and move to a city where you'll be forced to use silverware and eat off china plates that actually match. And you'll have no choice but to dry off after a shower with towels that are pretty as well as functional." She sighed dramatically. "I'll bet you envy me, getting to stay here and shoot pool with these icons of culture."

Ross looked at her, let his memory soak in the comfortable sight of Ellie, with her dark hair braided, her brown eyes alight with a familiar laughter, her wondrous smile not quite hidden by the teasing line of her lips. "Yeah," he said. "Lucky you."

Her gaze flicked to him and then returned to the three-way game getting set up in front of them. "Yes," she answered. "Lucky me."

Chapter Four

Ross dropped onto the sofa as if he meant to stay. "Got any popcorn?"

"What are you? A starving country?" Ellie slumped into the chair across from him, draping her legs over the cushioned arm. "You've practically eaten me out of house and home already. How can you stay so lean and eat like you do?"

"Pure thoughts." He looped an arm across the cushions and put his feet up.

"Impure thoughts is more like it."

He shrugged. "Those, too. So, what about the popcorn?"

"Microwave popcorn is in the cabinet next to the stove…right where we've always kept it." She watched him stand and head for the kitchen. "Set it for two minutes, ten seconds, not the three minutes it says on the bag or else it'll burn."

"Two minutes, ten seconds, or the popcorn's

toast. Got it.'' His voice coasted back to her, followed by the sound of the microwave door opening and closing and then the melodic beeps as he punched in the cook time. "You want me to put in a bag for you, too?"

She knew there was no point in suggesting he share his bag with her. In or out of love, Ross ate enough for two. "No, thanks," she called. "I'm not hungry."

"Aha!" He returned to the doorway between the two rooms. "Obviously you have not been thinking pure thoughts."

"I'll have you know my thoughts are every bit as pure as yours. They just don't do much for my appetite."

"Just as I suspected, Eliot. Your thought levels are seriously out of balance and you need a strong dose of *impure* thoughts to put your life back on an even keel."

"My life is perfectly *keeled*, thank you."

He raised his eyebrows in a familiar and charming expression. "It is only my professional opinion, of course, but I believe that if you asked him, Shorty would be delighted to help you make adjustments. It's pretty obvious he's still having impure thoughts about you, even if your thoughts about him are pure as the drizzled snow."

"*Driven* snow," she corrected. "And Shorty's too nice a man to have impure thoughts."

"Ellie!" He made a *tsk*-ing noise. "No man is that nice. Don't be fooled by his lanky Barry Manilow looks and shy demeanor. Underneath his plaid work shirt beats a heart as black as my own." Ross paused to consider. "Well, maybe not *that* black, but you get the idea."

"Living in the Windy City has made you cynical, Ross. Shorty is a nice man and I might go out with him sometime. If he ever gets up the courage to ask me again."

"Oh, come on, Eliot. You don't want to date a *nice* guy."

She lifted her eyebrows. "Why not? If all men have hearts as black as tar, then Shorty is at least as good as the rest of you. And undoubtedly better than most."

"I never said black as tar." The testy tone returned to Ross's voice. "You have nothing in common with Shorty Silvers. He does construction work, for Pete's sake."

Her eyebrows climbed a little higher. "And your point is…?"

His gaze dropped, but returned with the slightest touch of embarrassment. "I only meant he's not good enough for you, Ellie. You need a man with a little more depth, a little more ambition."

She had to look twice to make sure he was serious. "Oh, come on, Ross. I'm an auto mechanic. If I'm too good for a *nice* man who works with his hands in a respectable profession, then your idea of a match made in heaven differs considerably from mine.''

His easygoing smile fell victim to a glower. ''If you feel that way, why didn't you accept his invitation to be his date at the wedding? Why don't you just call him right now and tell him you've changed your mind?''

Ellie clamped her lips on the impulse to do just that, to pick up the phone and show Ross he was being ridiculous. ''I'm *your* date until four o'clock on Saturday. If I start having impure thoughts about Shorty or any other man, I'll have plenty of time to pursue them after I get you out of my hair.''

Whatever Ross meant to reply—and he *did* mean to reply, Ellie could tell just by the way he squared his jaw—was interrupted by the *beep, beep, beep* of the pager he wore attached to his belt. He clicked it off without even checking the message. ''May I use your phone?''

Ellie made a face, telling him via expression that he certainly didn't need her permission to call his fiancée. Tori had paged him four times while they were at The Wild Mouse. He'd called her back immediately each time…and each time returned cheerfully for another challenge at the pool table. Out of half a dozen attempts to win one game, he'd managed to lose not only his socks, but a handful of quarters, as well.

Ellie listened without compunction as he dialed the number.

"Hi," he said, his voice deepening to the husky tones of *Ross in love*.

Five seconds of listening came next, followed by a slight impatience in the sentimental tones as he replied, "No, now I'm at Ellie's.... No...just me and Ellie." A pause, then he said, "I don't know. They were still playing pool when I left.... I left with Ellie, yes."

Ellie stared at the ceiling, remembering the time Belinda had come looking for Ross, certain she'd find him with Ellie. Which she had. They'd been working on the Land Cruiser and hadn't even realized how late it was. Or how much fun they were having. Until Belinda showed up.

"That isn't necessary... No, really...I'm fine. I won't be long," Ross promised, turning his back so Ellie couldn't eavesdrop on the conclusion of the call. Not that she had any problem filling in the *I love you, too,* and the *I miss you, too,* ending for herself. She'd done it plenty of times before.

"Tori." He gave the one-word explanation as he hung up the phone...as if Ellie might not know who he'd called.

"Hmm." She let her lips curve just enough so

he'd know what she thought, even if she didn't say it.

And he knew. She could tell by the flash of irritation in his eyes. "She was worried that I might need a designated driver to get home safely."

Ellie nodded...and kept the Mona Lisa smile. "That was thoughtful."

"Yes." He rubbed the back of his neck as if it truly ached. "Tori is very thoughtful."

"Hmm." Ellie kept nodding and smiling. "Do you?"

"Do I what?"

"Need a ride home?"

He eyed her consideringly. "Maybe. I did have a few beers."

"No, you didn't. I watched you carry that one bottle around all evening, and if you took a single swallow, I certainly didn't see you."

"That's because you were making eyes at Shorty."

"Oh, that's right." She glanced at her wrist, as if checking the time. "I wonder if I should call to make sure *he* has enough sense to call a cab."

Ross frowned. "Tori's just being thoughtful," he said in her defense.

"Of course, she is. I wasn't implying that she was being anything else."

The microwave chimed, but Ross didn't move. He just stood there, looking at her, and for a moment, Ellie wanted to walk over and slug him for not having enough sense to know he was about to marry the wrong woman.

"She's just worried about me, that's all."

"I believe you."

"Like hell you do."

"You're the one who brought it up," Ellie pointed out. "The popcorn's ready."

Still, he didn't turn to go. "She's very busy this week. But she still cares enough to want to know what I'm doing and who I'm with."

Ellie's opinion of Tori inched up. For a nitwit, she was doing a good job of keeping Ross under her thumb. Pushing out of the armchair, Ellie walked into the kitchen, retrieved the bag of popcorn from the microwave and thrust it into his hands. "Here. You can feed your thoughts on your way home," she said.

He looked from the bloated bag to her. "I'd just as soon feed them while I sit and talk to you, if you don't mind."

"*My* mind is not the one that matters. You're engaged, Ross. Tori naturally wants you to be with her as much as possible and not with another woman."

"You're not another woman, Ellie. You're my best friend. Tori knows that."

The speed of his reply was somewhat daunting, but it wasn't as if their friendship revolved around the difference in their genders, after all. Well, a couple of times on her part, maybe, but she wasn't about to mention those.

Ross plunged his hand into the popcorn. "I even told her about the time I wanted to be more than your friend and that didn't seem to bother her."

"What time?"

He tossed a couple of popped kernels into his mouth and chewed with maddening nonchalance. "Didn't I ever mention that to you?"

"I think I would have remembered." She crossed her arms and leaned against the counter, her pulse picking up for no good reason. "So when, exactly, did you ever think about being more than my friend?"

He shrugged. "I can't really recall."

"Oh, no, you don't." She reached out and grabbed his arm when he would have turned away, drawing him back to the doorway, back to the point. "If you ever want to see your socks again, you'll tell me now and you'll tell me the truth."

"I never noticed this ruthless streak in you before, Eliot." He tapped her on the end of the nose and started for the sofa, munching popcorn as he went.

Ellie couldn't believe he'd done that. Tapped her on the nose as if she was an adoring puppy. Like she was *Tori!* Before she quite realized what she meant to do, Ellie had grabbed for a non-weapon and flung it at his broad and cocky shoulders. The stuffed purple bunny hit him square in the middle of the back and flopped harmlessly to the floor.

Ross turned slowly, his dark gold eyebrows arched in surprise, a fluffy piece of popcorn perched between his thumb and forefinger and held a bare inch from his mouth. His gaze dropped from Ellie to the floor, then with an annoying lack of response, he bent to pick up Purple Bunny. "Hey, I haven't seen this little guy in a while," he said as he lifted the tattered, flop-eared, one-eyed, half-stuffed rabbit off the floor. Turning the bunny over, Ross dusted him off, as if a bit of carpet fuzz would stand out amid all the stains the toy had accumulated over the years. "I see he's still sporting his Pat Paulsen For President! button."

"He's a lifetime member of the League of Women Voters, too," Ellie said on a sigh, wishing she hadn't thrown the toy at Ross, wishing he didn't know so much about the significance of Purple Bunny. The stuffed rabbit had come into her life through Lana and Kelly. None of them could really remember who had originally given the gift to whom, but it had become Lana's and Kelly's lucky charm and, when it was her turn to keep him, Purple Bunny became just one more thing Ellie had to keep track of. Not that she wasn't fond of the little fella. She just didn't like anyone else knowing she could be that sentimental.

Except Ross knew.

She could usually fool Lana and Kelly with her grumbling about believing a dumb bunny could bring luck, but Ross knew. Damn it, he knew. "Lana's had him the past several months and I sort of hoped she'd forget about passing him on to me, but over the weekend, at her wedding, she tossed him to me and, idiot that I am, I caught him."

"I'd have caught him, too, if I'd known you were going to toss him at me. That's no way to treat an old friend, El, and you know it." Ross held Purple Bunny against his chest, ignoring the miscellaneous clutter of nostalgia pinned to the ratty fur. "I take it you wanted to get my attention."

Ellie lifted her chin. "Don't tap me on the nose like you're my benevolent great uncle or something. You know how I feel about that sort of thing."

He frowned. "You didn't used to be so touchy."

"You didn't used to be so—" She stopped right there. Was she *trying* to pick a fight with him? When their time together was already on short notice? "Look, it's late. Maybe you ought to go home." Her glance fell to the bag of popcorn in his hand. "Take the popcorn with you and go home to your fiancée. Before she shows up here to get you."

There was a flicker of concern in his eyes, as if for an instant, he weighed love against friendship and wondered if he might have to choose between them. But then he dropped onto the sofa again, letting Purple Bunny slide down to sit beside him. So there they sat, the two men in her life. One almost out of stuffing and the other stuffing himself with popcorn. For all their shortcomings, she loved them both. With a shake of her head, she plopped herself into the shabby comfort of the armchair, where she could keep an eye on them.

But it seemed only fair to offer a warning. "She will come after you, Ross."

"No, she won't." His smile was the thing Ellie loved best of all. Mischievous, sexy, devil-may-care. He tossed more popcorn in his mouth and looked around. "So, tell me about Lana's wedding to... Who did she marry?"

"Blake Warner," Ellie supplied. "You'll like him, Ross. He's a really nice guy."

"He'd have to be if Lana married him. But I always thought she and Johnny were a match made in heaven."

"So did everyone else. Me included." She stretched out her hand and he, obligingly, put some popcorn in it. "But heaven-made matches come in a distant second to Las Vegas ones, it seems." Ellie related the tale of how prim-and-proper Lana had left to marry her childhood sweetheart, gotten stranded and pregnant in Las Vegas, and returned to Bachelor Falls sans any sign of Johnny and followed promptly by Blake. "You should have been here last month," Ellie concluded. "The Bachelor Falls busybodies were working overtime trying to find Lana's baby a proper father."

"Are you sure the Bostians didn't abduct the Lana we know and substitute someone more adventurous? I would never have thought Lana would... But I suppose, all's well that ends well, huh?" With a shake of his head, he tossed more popcorn into his mouth. "So, when's the baby due?"

"August."

"A baby, wow. That's hard to imagine. I'm sure Lana will be a wonderful mom—more like your mother than mine, I hope—but well, you know what I mean."

"It isn't like we're all still eighteen, Ross. You

said it yourself tonight. 'There comes a time for a man to settle down,' you said.'' She swallowed a piece of popcorn in her mouth, sucking off the saltiness. ''Even Kelly's getting married next month.''

''I heard. You're going to have to get on the stick, Ellie. Otherwise you'll end up being named honorary aunt to all your friends' kids.''

''Except yours. I'd have to be called Kaunt Ellie to match your three darling little K-kiddies.''

He shifted uncomfortably, knocking Purple Bunny into a floppy lump beside him. ''Tori gets a little carried away with her planning. We've barely even talked about having kids.''

Ellie arched her eyebrows playfully. ''You're having three children, Ross. One boy, one girl, one undecided. You might get to name the dog, but I wouldn't count on it.''

He set the bag of popcorn aside and propped Purple Bunny upright again. ''I'm not going to spend the entire week defending Tori every time you don't agree with something she says. So let's just get this out in the open right now and put it behind us. Because, come Saturday, I'm getting married.''

And that pretty much summed up the one thing she disagreed with most, Ellie thought. But instead of saying so, she just shook her head. ''One of the great things about our friendship has always been that we can disagree with impunity. There's nothing you need to defend to me. If you love Tori, then I'll love her, too. It's that simple."

"But...?"

That was the problem with having a friend who knew you so well. They could see through a lie at forty paces. "No *buts*. You're getting married and I'll adjust to the idea. I will."

He honestly looked surprised by the thought that his decision effected her. "Are you upset because I'm marrying Tori?"

"*Upset* is too strong a word, Ross." *Concerned, worried, annoyed*...any one of those would have been acceptable. But *upset?* No, she was not upset. "I'm a little—"

"Concerned?" he suggested.

"No," she lied, then blundered on before he could question it. "It's not that I expected you to stay single forever, you know. I intend to get married someday, myself. It's just knowing that we're both changing and our friendship is going to have to change, too."

He reached for the bag, but his hand paused in middive for more popcorn. "You worry too much," he said finally. "You and I go back too far and know too many of each other's secrets to lose touch. Fifty years from now, our friendship will be as strong as ever, you'll see. I'll even convince Tori that we should name the undecided child after you. T. S. Eliot Kilgannon has a nice ring to it, doesn't it?''

"Not enough *K*s," she said, remembering the times she'd daydreamed of how it might feel to have that name as her own. Not that she'd ever really thought it possible. She frowned as she noticed he'd begun rubbing his neck again as if it ached. "What's wrong with you?"

"I like a little variety in my alphabet. So sue me."

"No, what's wrong with your *neck?* You keep rubbing at it like it really hurts."

"Just a muscle spasm. It's been acting up more than usual the past few months."

About three and a half months, would be Ellie's guess. The exact amount of time he'd been engaged to Tori. But she wasn't going to point that out.

She didn't have to. "It's been getting worse ever since Tori and I set the date. All the extra stress of planning a wedding, I imagine." He stopped rubbing his neck and reached into the bag for more popcorn.

Ellie sighed and wrestled her way up from the depths of the armchair. She walked to the old desk in the corner, the one her mother used as a catchall for anything and everything she didn't know where else to put. Finding what she was looking for, Ellie walked over and put it next to Ross on the sofa. "There," she said. "Maybe that will help."

He looked at the small, plastic cow and munched some more popcorn. "I'll bet your fingers are really tired by the time you get a gallon of milk out of her," he said with a grin.

"I use a milking machine." She picked up the cow and showed him the rollers underneath. "It's a massager," she explained. "I thought it might help that pain in your neck."

He ran the plastic massager across the back of his neck in a quick experiment. "You're right. I can feel the pain beginning to *moo*-ve away."

"Give me that!" She took it from his hand, resolutely refusing to smile at his nonsense. "This is the way you do it." She knelt beside him on the sofa and used the massager to knead his shoulder muscles with short, rolling strokes. "See?"

"Mmm." Ross closed his eyes and leaned forward, turning slightly so she could reach a larger area of his back. "Must be a one-owner massager," he said. "Old Bessie didn't respond this well to me. Can you get her to graze just a little lower?"

Moving the massager in lower circles across his shoulders, Ellie laid her hand on his arm to brace herself as she leaned closer. The muscles in his arm flexed hard beneath her touch and her palm grew warm against his skin. She found a soft, stealthy pleasure in the repetitive, even motion and a faint fascination with the slow, steady rise and fall of Ross's back as he breathed in and out. In. Out.

"You could make a good living doing this, Ellie," he said, his voice relaxing into a deeper baritone. "How come you never told me you have hidden talents?"

"Same reason I never told you about the time I thought I wanted us to be more than friends."

He tensed beneath the back and forth motion of the massager and opened his eyes. "When was that?"

She pushed against his arm, feeling the corded strength under her fingertips, and sat back on her heels, dropping the cow massager into Purple Bunny's lap. "When was what?" she asked, all innocence.

He frowned at her and again set the popcorn bag aside. "When did you look upon my handsome visage and realize your heart was mine for the asking?"

Ellie wrinkled her nose. "Oh, it happened a long, long time ago. Before you had a *visage* at all. And, truth be known, I believe it was the time you introduced me to Freda's blackberry wine."

He grinned, probably as much with affection for the Kilgannon's longtime housekeeper and cook as at the remembered—and overly nostalgic—taste of her homemade liquors. "You're pulling my strings, Miss T. S. Eliot Applegate. And that is not a nice thing to do to a man who is willing to admit he once found you so irresistible he broke up with his girlfriend, only to learn to his dismay that you preferred a much inferior male."

Ellie looked at him, surprised and wantonly pleased. "You are such a liar, Ross."

"If I was going to lie about something like that, Ellie, believe me, I'd paint myself in a more flattering light."

The undertone of truth unaccountably made her uncomfortable. "Which supposedly inferior male did I prefer?"

"I've blocked the weasel's name from my memory," he said, smiling slyly as he crunched on a popcorn kernel. "It's too painful to recall. But I do remember the woman I scorned for you."

"Oh, I'll just bet you do." Ellie shifted her weight and stretched her legs until her bare feet rested on the coffee table. "Considering that you were always the one to break up with your girlfriends, you could name any one of them and be reasonably safe from argument."

"It was Stacy Halloran," he said, as if there could be no doubt. "I broke her heart and then..." He paused to sigh before popping another kernel into his mouth. "...and then you broke mine."

The ease of long familiarity returned as quickly as it had vanished and Ellie was once again comfortable with his teasing. "As I remember, you broke up with Stacy Halloran and started dating Belinda Morgan the very next day."

"Belinda was strictly rebound. I never really loved her."

"You never *really* loved any of them, Ross." She laughed. "Remember the time you were determined to elope with—oh, jeez, what *was* her name?"

He looked pleasantly blank. "Give me a hint. What did she look like?"

Ellie crossed her arms and gazed at him with amused patience. "Let's see if I can remember," she teased. "Short, blond, big blue eyes...does that ring any bells?"

He stopped smiling. "You just described Tori," he said in his let's-not-go-there tone of voice.

"I just described a girl you were passionately in love with during Christmas break of our junior year in high school. You surely see some similarities between the girls you've dated and the one you're going to marry?''

He put the empty popcorn bag on the table and dusted his hands on his jeans. ''Not really. Coloring, maybe. I've always been partial to blondes, I suppose, but you don't have to act as if they were all interchangeable.''

Ellie stared at him. ''That was not my meaning at all, Ross, and you know it.''

He held her gaze for a moment and, for the first time, Ellie considered the possibility that their friendship had already changed, had already veered onto a path which would take them away from each other.

''You'd be perfectly within your rights to boot me off your comfy sofa, Eliot.'' Ross's eyes held an apology, as well as a plea for peace. ''I don't know why I'm suddenly so sensitive over every little thing you say about Tori. The only explanation I can offer is that it's terribly important to me that the two of you get along.''

''It's important to me, too, Ross.''

''So you're not going to kick me off the couch?''

She shook her head. ''I've already beat your socks off tonight. So I'm feeling rather gracious. When I want you to leave, I'll point at the door and you'll go.''

He put his hand over hers, there on the cushion, with Purple Bunny as chaperone, and Ellie felt a shiver of longing twist deep inside her heart. Once he'd thought of her as more than a friend. Once—or twice—she'd thought of him as a friend who might become something more. But their *once* had never coincided and for just a moment she wondered what might have happened if it had.

Of course, this was better. She'd trade a dozen what-ifs for the certainty that Ross was, and always would be, her friend. "I think maybe we're both feeling a little threatened by what marriage will do to our relationship. It has to change, you know. It wouldn't be fair to Tori if it didn't."

"I know." He squeezed her hand and picked up the popcorn bag. "Popcorn's gone."

"It's late."

He looked at her hopefully. "One more bag?"

"Ross..."

"Thanks, Ellie. You're saving me from certain starvation." He got up and headed for the kitchen, crumpling the empty bag into a ball, tossing it in the air and catching it with one hand. "Got anything to drink with it? Some milk, maybe?"

"I milked the cow just this morning," she called after him, more glad than she wanted to admit that he was in no hurry to go home to his fiancée. "Check the fridge."

As he disappeared into the kitchen, Ellie heard the aggressive buzz of a sports car as it turned onto the block and zipped down the street, passing the house in fourth gear. From the kitchen, she heard Ross set the microwave and open the refrigerator, whistling as he prepared his snack. Outside, the car braked, its gears grating as it suddenly backed down the street nearly as fast as it had gone up. Ellie watched the twin headlights cut a swatch of light across the porch and heard the sudden quiet as the motor whirred to an abrupt stop in her driveway. With a sigh, she picked up Purple Bunny and arranged his long, sad ears. "Your designated driver is here," she called to Ross.

He stopped whistling and appeared in the doorway a second later. "What?"

"Tori's here."

He looked momentarily dismayed, his gaze switching from Ellie to the door and back. "What's she doing here?"

"Just a guess," Ellie said dryly, "but I imagine she's merely being *thoughtful*."

Ross met and held her gaze.

"Or maybe she wanted to make sure popcorn was all we were sharing."

There was no guilty start, no blink of surprise, nothing to indicate that the same idea hadn't occurred to him as well. "She doesn't eat popcorn," he said.

Ellie didn't comment. She just gave Purple Bunny an unenthusiastic tap on his frayed nose and went to open the door for Tori.

Chapter Five

"Where'd you pick up the Beamer?" Chip asked when Ellie walked into the office the next morning. "Thought you didn't hold with foreign-made cars."

"It beats walking."

"And every other means of getting to work." Chip moved himself and his admiration to the window. "How come you're driving Ross's car?"

Dropping the keys onto her desk, Ellie glanced at the shiny, black BMW she'd just parked out front. "It was blocking my driveway this morning."

Chip turned to look at her with a huge grin, obviously imagining only one trade worthy of getting to drive the BMW. "Is he sleeping over at your house?"

Ellie sighed, the grumpiness that had plagued her all morning coming at her again in a rush.

"No, Chip, he isn't sleeping over. He left the car at my house last night and rode home with his fiancée. I told him I'd drive it to work this morning and he could pick it up here."

"Want me to take it to him?" he asked eagerly.

"No, thanks. It isn't as if we don't have plenty of empty parking spaces." She paused, narrowing her gaze on the sleek and sporty import. "Unless you think it might scare off our regular customers?"

"Well, your uncle Owen won't like it much," Chip said, then brightened with the lightbulb of an idea. "But I could move it around back, if you want. That way he wouldn't see it."

Ellie smiled. "Uncle Owen isn't likely to come by this morning. I'm sure the car will be fine right where I left it."

Chip moved a little closer to the window and for a minute, Ellie thought he might press his nose to the glass like the little boy he still sometimes seemed to be. "Man, what I wouldn't give to drive a sweet automobile like that."

"Go to college." Ellie repeated the advice she offered him at least once a day, whether he asked for it or not. "Get a degree. Become a doctor. Then you can buy yourself pretty much whatever *sweet* vehicle your little heart desires."

"Be easier to have rich parents." Chip sighed. "Tell me what it's like to drive a car like that."

"It's…great," she answered truthfully. "But it isn't *that* great. Call me old-fashioned, but I still prefer my El Camino."

"If you'd paint the Chevy, you could be old-fashioned *and* be driving a real car." Chip turned his lanky length away from the window and tried a different tack. "If *I* had a classic like the Chevy, I'd invite Emily Matthews to the Falls Day dance Friday night and I'll bet she'd go, too."

"I thought you already had a date with Sarah."

"Well, yeah. But she's just a friend."

Ellie looked up from the stack of invoices on her desk. "Are you telling me that if I offered to loan you the Chevy for that one night, you'd ditch your good friend and ask some little blonde with big blue eyes to go in her place?"

"Well…yeah." His shrug was clearly unrepentant. "Emily's a cheerleader."

"Oh, well, in that case, I'm sure Sarah would understand completely." Ellie crammed the invoices into the top drawer and slammed it shut. "Men," she said. "You're all alike, no matter what age you are."

Chip looked at her as if she were nuts. "If you offered to let Sarah borrow the Chevy, she'd drop

me like a hot potato and ask Robert Perkins to
go with her.''

"Would she, really?" Ellie considered the
possibility, aggravated beyond reason with
Chip's attitude. "Let's just find out. What's her
number?"

"Emily's?" Chip's huge feet shifted toward
the door.

"No, Sarah's. You do know your good
friend's phone number, don't you?"

"Well, yeah, sure." Chip shuffled some more
and told her the number.

Feeling as if she was striking a blow for females everywhere, Ellie dialed and waited for
Sarah to answer. When she finally did, her voice
sounded seventeen and sleepy. Very sleepy.
"Sarah," Ellie said brightly. "Listen. I have a
question. If someone offered to loan you, oh, say
a classic Chevrolet coupe to drive to the dance
Friday night, who would you take?"

"Brad Pitt," Sarah said sleepily.

"No, not a fantasy date. Someone from Bachelor Falls."

"Oh." There was a pause. "I'm going with
Chip Jenkins."

"Aha," Ellie smiled broadly at Chip. "That's
what I thought."

There was a definite yawn at the other end of

the line. "What kind of car did you say some-one's going to loan me?"

"A 1957 Chevrolet coupe. A real classic."

"Oh. Any chance of getting something more modern?" Sarah was apparently approaching a state of consciousness. "If I had a really cool set of wheels, I could probably get Robert Perkins to take me to the dance."

Shot down, Ellie thought, and then wondered why in hell she was talking to two seventeen-year-olds about cars. As if they knew the value of a classic. Or of friendship, for that matter. "Here's Chip." She thrust the phone at him and he kept a wary eye on her as he approached the desk.

"Hi," Chip said into the mouthpiece, turning to muffle his side of the conversation from Ellie. "I don't know. She's being very weird."

Weird, Ellie thought. She was twenty-nine, racing toward thirty, and acting *weird* because two silly teenagers didn't appreciate the friend-ship they shared with each other. As if she cared who they took to the dance...or even whether they went or not. Ellie picked up Ross's keys and hung them on the Peg-Board beside her desk.

Okay, she admitted, so this isn't about Sarah and Chip at all. It's about Ellie and Ross...and Tori. Pushing away from her desk, she left the office and headed for the back bay of the garage.

Hot Rod was there, waiting for her like an old friend. A friend she could depend on, talk to, know she owned absolutely, forever. A friend no fiancée was going to accost at 1 a.m. and *rescue* from the extra calories and cholesterol in a simple bag of popcorn. Opening the door, she slid onto the seat and fit her hands around the steering wheel. It felt cool and solid beneath her palms. Uncle Owen had given it to her along with the garage. She paid him a pittance each month in exchange, but basically, he'd given them to her with his best wishes six years ago. Since then she'd lovingly restored each part of the car…with Ross sharing in every decision either when he was home on break or by long distance. She'd planned all along to paint the car candy apple red, no matter how many times she teasingly told him she wouldn't.

So now it was time to finish the job. Over time, her friendship with Ross was going to become one of distance and distractions. She wouldn't be able to call him with minor happenings in her life. The times they'd spent on the phone, talking into the wee hours of the night, were drawing to a close. But she'd still have Hot Rod to talk to any time of the day or night. And that was something she could count on.

"Tori probably hates classic cars," Ellie said aloud, her hands stroking the chrome steering wheel. Anyone who didn't eat sweets or popcorn or meat loaf wasn't going to be overly impressed with a '57 Chevy. Not that it mattered what Tori thought about the car. It was Ross's opinion that Ellie cared about. And she was going to make sure he enjoyed at least one ride in the hot rod before Tori brainwashed him into believing a Miata was a real car. Lovingly, Ellie patted the as-yet unpainted dashboard. "Today," she promised.

"Ellie?" Chip called from the front bay. "Miz Eubanks is here to see you. Says her Barracuda is making a strange noise again."

With a half smile, Ellie got out of the Chevy and gently closed the door. "Duty calls," she said, and went toward the office and the first customer of the day.

ROSS UNFOLDED HIMSELF from the low-slung interior of Tori's Miata, stifling the urge to shake himself like a wet dog. The Miata always gave him cramps in one way or another. But Tori loved it and it was a great-looking little car. *Little,* unfortunately, being the operative word. He walked around the car and leaned in the driver's side window to kiss Tori goodbye. "Watch out for my mother," he warned her with a smile. "She's not used to your kind of kamikaze shopping."

Tori shifted the car into Reverse as she puckered up and blew him a kiss. "I will return your mother to you this evening a wiser and more daring woman."

"Poorer," he said.

"Definitely poorer. See you tonight." She revved the motor as she waited for a brown UPS truck to rumble past, then gravel spun as the Miata peeled out of the parking lot and headed down Roosevelt Avenue looking something like a Chihuahua yapping at the heels of a Great Dane.

Ross watched as she cut out into the left lane and passed UPS with a full car-length to spare—if the Miata counted as a *full* car. Three seconds, max, was all that saved Thelma Perkins's Roadmaster from getting clipped on the left headlight. He didn't know why Tori had to drive as if there were no tomorrow, but he tried never to get in any car if she was behind the wheel. It wasn't the way he'd wanted to start this morning, that was for certain.

Glancing toward the office of Applegate Auto Repair, he saw Ellie looking out the front window, her eyebrows raised, one thumb resting in the tool loop of her overalls, one palm pressed against the pane. She was looking after the Miata with a frown, watching it disappear like a streak of red around the corner of Roosevelt and Wilson. Ross knew that look, and he knew he didn't want it turned on him. Because if Ellie looked at him now, he'd have to admit, either with a shrug or a grin, that Tori wasn't perfect. And he wasn't going to do that. Not this morning when his eyes were gritty from lack of sleep and his temper was on the short side of good humor. So, without another glance toward the window, he dodged the "look" and walked into the office as nonchalantly as if Mario Andretti had just dropped him off on his way to the Indianapolis 500.

"Hi, Mr. Kilgannon." Chip's smile was as lanky and loose as the rest of him. "You must be the luckiest man alive."

He felt cramped, not lucky, but Ross recognized teenage envy when he saw it. "Yes," he said. "I must be. Tori's a wonderful woman."

"Yeah." Chip turned another glance toward the parking lot. "A blonde, a BMW and a Miata. Man. You wouldn't want to loan me a set of wheels for Friday night's dance, would you?" He again gazed admiringly at the sleek little Beamer. "I could probably get Alison Hargrave to go out with me if I was driving something like that."

"I suppose she's a cheerleader, too?" Ellie spoke for the first time as she moved away from the window and behind her cluttered old desk.

"No, she's an older woman," Chip said on his

way out the side door. "A topless dancer over in Fayetteville."

Ross raised his eyebrows. "He's kidding, right?"

She looked after the boy with affectionate exasperation. "I think so, but with teenage boys it's hard to tell. I just gave him a hard time about standing up his good friend, Sarah, and lusting after Emily, the cheerleader. I suppose he wants me to worry a little about him and older women."

"Little does Chip know, you're not a worrier. Look at all the times I stood you up for some little nitwit with more blond than brains." Ross smiled, expecting a bit of roasting in return.

But Ellie didn't even smile. She flipped through her Rolodex with a studied concentration, as if she were hardly aware of Ross's presence. He felt a tweak of annoyance. He was only in town for a few days, damn it. She shouldn't be acting as if this was just like his other visits home. He was getting married on Saturday, for Pete's sake, and he needed her attention. "I'm driving up to Springfield this morning," he said conversationally.

"Mmm." Ellie flipped through a few more cards, rearranging one here and there. "*I* before *E* is a spelling rule, Chip," she said aloud, even though the boy wasn't anywhere within earshot. "*E* still comes before *I* in the alphabet."

"I need to get Tori a wedding-day present."

"There it is," Ellie said happily as she pulled a card from the file. "Granny's Body Shop."

"I was hoping you could go with me, help me pick out something special," Ross finished, a hint of irritation vying for control of his voice. "But if you're too busy…"

"Too busy for what?"

"To listen?" he suggested pointedly.

Ellie glanced at him, then looked again at the card in her hand. "I'm sorry. I was thinking about something else."

"Obviously."

This time her deep brown eyes focused fully on him, interested in a distracted, mysterious sort of way. "What?" she said, her gaze drifting to the phone card still clutched in her hand. "Did you ask me something important?"

He had the strangest impulse to reach across her desk and tip up her chin until she'd have to look him in the eye and listen to what he was saying. But she didn't like anyone touching her chin. No, it was her nose. She hadn't wanted him to tap her on the nose. "I did ask you something," he said, keeping his hands to himself. "And it is kind of important to me."

She nodded, but her gaze strayed back to the

card. "Could I just—?" Her tone held the confidence that he would, of course, understand. "It'll only take a minute."

He knew when to give in. "Why don't you call Granny and take care of whatever it is that's got you in such a dither? Then maybe you can spare me a few minutes."

Her smile flashed warm, wide and mesmerizing in its suddenness. "I don't get in a *dither,* Ross. You're confusing me with the other women in your life. Give me five minutes to take care of this and then I'm all yours." She picked up the phone and punched in the numbers. Her smile drifted from him to the card she still held in her hand, but still somehow claimed his interest.

All yours, he thought wryly. As if Ellie belonged to him in any way, shape or form. She was the most self-possessed person he'd ever met. Had been since the time he became aware of her existence in sixth grade, when, without preamble, she'd asked him to be her bodyguard. He'd never thought to ask why she'd chosen him when, at the time, he hadn't been much taller or scrappier than she was herself. And he'd never really thought about why he'd agreed to be her protector in exchange for a homemade chocolate chip cookie at lunchtime. Right now he couldn't even remember who he had protected her from...or even if she'd actually ever needed protecting. But that had been the beginning of their friendship and the first time he'd experienced the wonderfully powerful sensation of knowing someone needed him.

All yours, he thought. In lots of way, *he* belonged to Ellie. So many memories, so much of his life was wrapped up with hers. She knew things about him no one else would ever know. She'd been beside him at the best and worst moments of his life. She believed in him more fiercely than he believed in himself. And on top of it all, when she smiled at him, he knew that—at least in her eyes—he would always be someone very special. So in that way, and probably others he wasn't fully aware of, he *was* all hers. Not in a romantic way, of course. There never had been that between them…and now he wondered why.

True, she'd been something of a late bloomer. The first time he'd come home on break from college, he'd taken one look at his old friend and realized she wasn't one of the guys…in more ways than one. He couldn't put his finger on what had changed, but Ellie was suddenly different. Not precisely beautiful, but certainly striking. Not exactly a Playboy centerfold, but heads definitely turned when she walked by. At the time, Ross had entertained an assortment of purely lustful thoughts. He'd wanted to explore this new and unfamiliar Ellie. He'd even considered the possibility of convincing her to go back to Chicago with him, despite knowing that she was seriously in love with her electronics instructor. But then when she'd laughed and wanted to know if she'd suddenly developed a wart on her nose, the moment had passed, and she was once again the best friend he knew in the world.

As he watched her now, he wondered if they'd both subconsciously avoided the "something more" they occasionally felt, in order to preserve the one thing they were each certain of...that their friendship was the most cherished possession either of them possessed. Ross felt the warmth of his love for Ellie from the inside out as he watched her laugh and talk with whoever was on the other end of the phone line. Granny, he supposed.

"I can be there in an hour," she announced happily. "Promise you won't start another job before you can get to mine?" She laughed again, leaning her head back against the cracked chair cushion, exposing a long expanse of slender throat. "I know you've been waiting a year to do this, but... Okay, enough said. See you then." She hung up, still wearing that mysterious, disarming smile as she clasped her hands on top of her desk and leaned forward. "Okay, Ross. Ask me anything."

He stood there for a moment, watching her smile, then he put his palms on the desk and leaned toward her, until he was near enough to whisper. "Run away with me."

She laughed. "Don't have time. I've got to take Hot Rod to Springfield."

"Granny's Body Shop." Ross grinned, comprehending the gist of her phone call. "You're going to get the Chevy painted."

She shrugged. "I figured you should ride in a really *hot* car before you settle down to a life of mundane luxury. Paula Meyers has been dying to get her hands on Rod's body for months. It'll be close, but she promised he'd be ready for the Falls Day parade...*if* she can get started this morning."

Ellie pushed up and out of her chair and Ross noticed the full curves of her breasts beneath her habitual T-shirt and denim overalls. She did have a nice shape, he thought. And he'd always, privately, believed she had the best legs in town. Much more shapely than Belinda Morgan's skinny calves. "Why was it you never tried out for cheerleader?" he asked.

Ellie shot him a quick, astonished glance. "Do you want the long list or the short one?" She shook her head and her braid fell off her shoulder to dangle down her back. "I believe that's the dumbest thing you've ever said to me. What made you ask that now, for Pete's sake?''

Discretion was in order, for sure. Telling her she had great legs would only net him a suspicious, flattery-will-get-you-nowhere response. ''I was thinking about Belinda Morgan, that's all.''

Ellie pulled a Cardinals baseball cap off a hook on the wall and put it on. ''She still lives in Bachelor Falls, you know. I'm sure she'd be delighted to know you still think of her cheerleading costume with the same reverence you had in high school.''

Ross hated that Ellie could follow the track of his thoughts so easily. Even if she wasn't entirely accurate. ''I was thinking how scrawny her legs always were,'' he defended himself as he followed Ellie out of the office. ''And how great yours are.''

The right-left swing of her braid across her back indicated she was unimpressed with his compliment. ''Right. I suppose next you'll tell me you could pick my legs out of a lineup of women in short skirts.''

He followed her, falling easily into a well-remembered banter. ''So, does this mean you will run away with me?''

''Where are you going?''

''Springfield.''

She glanced over her shoulder. ''What a coincidence. That's where I'm going…but, unfortunately, I have to drive my own car so I won't be able to go with you.''

"You're going to need a ride back."

"I'll hitchhike," she said. "With my legs, it'll be no trouble at all."

"You'd better let me follow you to Granny's and bring you home," he said in a serious tone. "Because you'll never get those pant legs rolled up in time to stop a car."

"I'll stop on the way in and buy a dress."

"Mmm-hmm. Don't kid a kidder, Eliot. I know better than anyone how much you hate to wear dresses. You're just giving me a hard time, even though you know you're going to help me shop for Tori's wedding-day present."

Ellie stopped just outside the last bay and turned toward him. "*You're* going shopping?" she asked.

"I meant to get Tori's gift before I left Chicago, but it slipped my mind."

Her expression gave away nothing, but Ross knew what she was thinking and he wished he'd omitted the part about it having *slipped* his mind. "I need to check on the tuxedo rentals anyway, so I thought I'd just combine the two errands into one trip. Today. And I want you to go with me."

Ellie stared at him, her eyes assessing the hidden meaning. "If you think *I'm* going to pick out a present for you to give to your bride-to-be, you can just forget about it right now."

"I merely want the pleasure of your company," he said with only a twinge of guilt. "And...maybe your opinion about the gift."

"You don't have the faintest idea what to get her or where to look for it, do you?"

He frowned, knowing it was pointless to deny his lack of creativity when it came to a gift for his bride. "You're my best man, Ellie. It's your duty to help me. Besides, if we're both going to Springfield, we may as well have the pleasure of being with each other."

Her frown softened and faded behind a slow smile. "You always did have a way with words, Kilgannon. But I expect you to buy me lunch, understand?"

"Anything you want."

"I *want* to not go shopping."

He loved the way she made just the word *shopping* sound so disgusting. "It will be good for you. Trust me."

She eyed him consideringly from under the bill of her ball cap. "I want a frozen custard from Andy's before we come back, too."

"You drive a difficult bargain, El, but it's a deal. Lunch *and* frozen custard. Now, give Chip instructions on what to do and what not to do while you're gone. I'll follow you in the BMW and wait for you at Granny's.''

She hesitated, glancing absently at her left wrist. ''One more thing, I'm not going to spend all day shopping. I have to be home by six-thirty. No excuses.''

''None will be offered, believe me.'' He put his arm around her shoulders and they walked companionably into the back bay. ''After all, I'm the prospective groom. I can't miss my own surprise wedding shower tonight, now, can I?''

She frowned up at him. ''You're not supposed to know about that.''

He laughed. ''I'm a Bachelor Falls native, remember? How could I *not* know about the shower when everyone, including you, has gone out of their way to make certain I'll be in town at six-thirty?''

''Life in a small town,'' Ellie said with a shake of her head. ''Ain't it grand?''

''Yes,'' he agreed. ''Ain't it, though?''

Chapter Six

"How about this?" Ross held up a drab green T-shirt bearing the picture of a trout in a Revolutionary War uniform and stamped with the slogan War Of The Worms.

Ellie took it from him and dropped it with the other novelty shirts. "You are not going to find a wedding present for Tori in the Bass Pro Shop. Now quit stalling and let's go someplace where there's at least a remote possibility of locating an appropriate gift."

"Tori loves the great outdoors. I think she might like one of these shirts." He held up another—a navy with the same trout in bathing trunks and cap above the caption Swim With The Big Fish Or Stay Out Of The Stream! "This one's a good color for her."

"Even I wouldn't wear that," Ellie said. "You're wasting time, Ross. Let's go to the jewelry store and get this over with."

"Jewelry is so obvious." He took Ellie's hand and steered her purposefully from the sportswear to the exercise equipment. "I want to get something she'll always remember."

"There's remembering and then there's remembering." Ellie stopped in the middle of the aisle of the huge Bass Pro Shop and crossed her arms at her chest. "What you want, Ross, is for her to remember with genuine *pleasure.*"

Ross ignored her critical stance and checked the stats on a stair-stepping machine. He knew, of course, that it wasn't an appropriate wedding gift, but he hadn't been inside the sporting goods store in years and he wanted to look around. He also rather liked hearing that rising note of concern in Ellie's voice, as if she wasn't entirely sure he was teasing. It pleased him to think she couldn't always read his mind. "If Tori gave me a rowing machine or a set of weights, I'd think it was a great wedding present."

"No, you wouldn't." The note of concern vanished completely. "You're a romantic at heart, Ross, so stop trying to make me think you'd actually buy your beloved an exercise bike and let's go."

"For your information, Tori is an avid exerciser." He pretended intense interest in a rowing machine. "She'd love this."

"If she's besotted enough with you to accept

a contraption like that as a wedding gift, then the two of you deserve each other. I'm going back upstairs to the restaurant. You'll find me there with a cup of coffee when you're through piddling around.''

"Wait." He put his hand on her arm to stop her…and felt a startling backlash of response. He dropped his hand quickly, but the odd sensation didn't go away.

"What?" she asked. "This is a big place, but I won't be that far away. When you're ready to leave testosterone city, just come and get me. Okay?"

"Sure." He jammed his hand into his pants pocket and curled his fingers around the warmth in his still-tingling palm. "Go ahead. I won't be long."

She looked puzzled, but didn't ask him what was wrong. For which he was grateful, because he didn't have the faintest idea what had just happened. Or rather, he did have an idea…which was the problem. Watching Ellie walk toward the stairs and the restaurant three floors up, he took his hand from his pocket and then stared curiously at his palm. *You're getting married on Saturday. You're tense. You're stressed. You're imagining things.* He nodded, satisfied, and repeated the silent litany for good measure. *You're*

getting married on Saturday. You're tense.
You're stressed. You're imagining things.

That settled, he headed for the fishing tackle
and the relatively safe fantasies of the fish that
wouldn't get away.

ELLIE CAME UP BESIDE HIM in the middle of
Barnes & Noble. "You're not buying that for
her, either," she said, tapping the spine of the
Clancy novel in his hands.

"I have to have something to read on the honeymoon," he said, allowing her to see the pa-
perbacks he'd picked up as well. "And I'm getting these Iris House mysteries for Tori. Don't
you think she'll like that?"

"Does she like mysteries?"

"I don't know," he answered, realizing he'd
never seen Tori with a book of any kind. "She
likes magazines."

"Not exactly the same thing."

He sorted through the three titles he'd chosen
and looked hopefully at Ellie. "You like mysteries."

"Yes, and I particularly like Hager's Iris
House series, but I'm not Tori and this isn't my
honeymoon."

"So, what would you want to read if it were?"

Her smile was slow and sexy enough to knock
the stuffing out of a lesser man. "Erotica," she

said. "Supposing, of course, that I wanted to *read* at all." Turning, she meandered down the aisle, leaving Ross a bit weak in the knees.

"THANKS," ELLIE SAID as she took the cone of frozen custard and scooted over so Ross could sit beside her on the curb. Andy's Frozen Custard was a small operation, offering a great product in several different forms, but not many places to sit and lick. "What did you get?"

"Strawberry-banana. Want a lick?"

She leaned across him and her tongue made a clean swipe across his custard. Using the back of her hand, she blotted her lips. "Good," she said and held out her cone. "Try mine."

"I know what vanilla tastes like, Ellie." They had this same exchange every time they came into Springfield, because they always stopped at Andy's and she always got a vanilla cone. Always. "Wonder if I could get Tori a gift certificate for frozen custard as a wedding present?"

"Custard would pollute her arteries."

His gaze cut to Ellie and she shrugged apologetically. "I'm only guessing, of course. Tori might really like Andy's custard."

"She wouldn't touch it. You're right." He slid a spoonful of the rich treat into his mouth and wondered how he had fallen in love with a woman who wouldn't taste frozen custard on a bet. "I guess we'll hit the jewelry store right after we stop at the tuxedo rental place," he said sadly.

She scooped a mouthful of custard onto her tongue, swallowed, and savored the moment by licking her lips. "If it makes you feel any better, I think an Andy's gift certificate is an inspired idea. Just in case you were wondering what to get me for a best-man present."

"I'll keep that in mind." He leaned forward to avoid a drip and settled in to enjoy the frozen custard, the sun-warmed curb and Ellie's company.

IN THE DRESSING ROOM of Springfield Formal Wear, Ellie faced the mirror and her first experience with a tuxedo. The cummerbund drooped over her waist and needed to be tightened. The slacks hung loose and straight around her thighs, the crotch sagged, but the material was slightly snug around the hips. The pleated shirt puckered down the front instead of lying flat across her breasts and the bow tie needed to be about three inches shorter around her neck. The arms of the jacket hung nearly to her fingertips and there was no way she would ever be able to wear those shoes. This was a mistake, she thought. Why had she ever agreed to be Ross's best man? As if it wasn't going to be bad enough standing next to him while he vowed to love, honor and cherish a nitwit, now she'd have to do it knowing she looked like a tomboy next to Tori's feminine bridal white.

With a frown, Ellie tugged the band from the end of her braid and pulled on the entwined strands until her hair rained about her shoulders in a heavy shower of dark waves. The tuxedo still looked odd and ill-fitting, and it was nowhere near as comfortable as her overalls, but at least she felt sure she wouldn't be mistaken for Ross's little brother.

"Let me see, please." The tailor clapped his hands outside her cubicle and Ellie, reluctantly, parted the curtains and stepped out. Ross was standing a few feet away, looking heart-stoppingly handsome in white tie and tails that couldn't possibly need much, if any, alteration. His eyes met hers in the triple mirror and he smiled, slowly, as if he couldn't believe what he was seeing.

"I haven't seen you wear your hair like that since the night of our junior prom."

She wrinkled her nose at him…and the memory. "Oh, thanks for reminding me," she said as the tailor, a Mr. Spleare, positioned her like a tree with arms outstretched and legs apart, while he tugged and tucked and pinned. "I hope I never have another night as embarrassing as that one."

Ross laughed. "Promise me you won't decide

to give yourself a perm Friday night before the wedding?"

"It was a reverse perm, guaranteed to straighten even the curliest hair." Her voice squeaked on the last word as Mr. Spleare fore-shortened the seat of her trousers. "And believe me, I'll *never* do that again."

"Good." Ross's tone deepened to a throaty and sentimental baritone. "Because I love your hair...just the way it is."

"PEARLS ARE NICE. But, of course, we know that brides always love diamonds." The jewelry store clerk was all smiles as she followed Ross from counter to counter, where he considered and dis-carded suggestions as if he had the rest of his life to find Tori's gift.

Ellie perched on a high-backed stool, her el-bows braced on the glass countertop behind her, her overall-clad legs wrapped around the wooden legs of the stool. In the display case beneath her elbows was an assortment of pearl rings, neck-laces, broaches and pendants. There was one par-ticularly lovely bracelet, but Ellie was waiting for the opportune moment to suggest it as perfect for Tori. At the moment, Ross seemed bent on choosing a gift without benefit of counsel.

"Let's look at the watches again," he said to the clerk, who somehow managed to keep on smiling. "I especially like the one with the odd-shaped dial."

"It is unusual." The clerk unlocked the case and pulled out the watch.

Ellie didn't even wander over to take a second look. It was wearable art, with eye-catching, abstract details and a price tag that made a Rolex seem like a bargain. And Tori would hate it. Ellie had known that the moment she saw it, but for some reason, Ross kept going back to it.

"I think this is it," he said decisively. "Don't you agree, El?"

She frowned at him across two display cases and a turntable of half-price earrings. "No, Ross, I don't. You coerced me into this shopping trip by saying you needed my opinion. So I'm going to give it to you. Tori will hate that watch."

"How do you know?"

"I just do."

His jaw flexed, irritably. "I think I know my fiancée a little better than you do."

"I certainly hope so, but if you honestly believe she'll wear that watch, much less treasure it for the rest of her life, you know a lot less about her than you think."

"I'm taking the watch."

"Come over here and look at this bracelet first," she suggested. "It has *Tori* written all over it."

"It is a beautiful piece and there is a matching necklace." The clerk all but tossed the watch back into its case before she hurried around to open the display behind Ellie. "Pearls just seem to go with brides, you know. Why just the other day, I sold a gorgeous set of pearls—necklace, bracelet and earrings—to a young man as a gift for his bride."

The bracelet pooled in Ross's large palm like frozen, salty teardrops, then he held it out to Ellie. "Try it on, please."

Wordlessly, she offered her wrist and the clerk draped the pearls around it. The bracelet felt surprisingly heavy as Ellie turned her hand, palm out, then in, to show Ross how the light affected the dappled white of the pearls. "See?" she said. "It's a beautiful bracelet."

"But you prefer the watch."

It was a statement, not a question at all, but she answered him anyway. "Yes, Ross, I like the watch. But Tori won't. I'm right about this. Buy her the bracelet."

He frowned and looked at the clerk, who nodded a wholehearted and relieved agreement. "It's the perfect gift for the perfect bride," she said.

"All right." Ross grudgingly capitulated to the female majority. "Gift wrap the bracelet...and give the watch to her." He indicated

Ellie with a jerk of his head. "She'll wear it home."

Ellie's feet slipped off the rung of the stool. "What did you say?"

"I'm buying the watch for you."

"Ross! You can't do that. It's much too expensive. It costs more than Tori's bracelet, even."

"That part we won't tell her, but I'm buying you that watch. Think of it as a thank-you for the gift of your friendship."

The clerk's face was wreathed in a smile and she eyed Ellie with new interest. "Oh, that's so sweet."

"And completely out of the question," Ellie said. "I can't accept it."

"Yes, you can." The stubborn glint in his green eyes informed her there was no point in arguing further. So she didn't. "I'd have been just as happy with the gift certificate from Andy's," she said as they walked out of the store a little while later.

"I know," he said and opened the car door for her. "But this way, every time you look at your wrist, you'll think of me."

She checked her wrist, where the gold and silver band reflected sunlight in a shower of flashy rays. "What do you know? It works."

"If it ever doesn't, we're taking it back."

"I meant, it made me think of you."

He smiled down at her, catching her heart by surprise. "That's what I meant, too."

Ellie swallowed the sentimental lump in her throat as she slid into the passenger seat. "It would have cost a lot less and I'm pretty sure I'd have thought of you every time I used my Andy's gift certificate, too."

"But you wouldn't have been able to give me the time of day." He grinned and stepped back to close the door. "Holy moley," he said. "I feel a *song* coming on."

"REMEMBER THIS ONE?" Ross tapped an introductory rhythm on the steering wheel, then sang a couple of preliminary *doo-wap, doo-waps,* before he belted out a melodious, "'Love is like an antique car…it can't take you too far. Just when you're rollin' along…your heart singin' a song…the engine shuts down…you're stranded out of town. Shut down. Shut down. Shut down by love. Shut down. Shut down. Put down by love.'"

Ellie laughed with him at the song they'd composed one long-ago night after a particularly traumatic broken heart. "I can't believe we actually wrote that one down."

"I can't believe some hot country singer hasn't picked up the option on it. I've always felt, deep in my heart, that 'Shut Down' could have been a classic.''

"Funny, I can remember the song, but not who broke my heart.'' She pondered the mystery and watched the green Missouri landscape unfold by the mile as Ross drove steadily toward home.

"Harlen Daniels,'' Ross said after a few seconds of consideration. "He left a message on *my* answering machine and I had to go over to your house to tell you that I was right all along and Harlen really was a jerkface.''

"Oh, yes, I remember now.'' The memory came back to Ellie in sketchy detail. "Harlen was a jerkface and, in my hour of misery, you kept calling your house and letting me hear the message over and over again so I'd understand what a jerkface he was and stop crying.''

Ross nodded. "That's just the kind of sensitive guy I am. On the other hand, I did bring along a couple packs of Fig Newtons and my guitar.''

She laid her head against the leather head rest. "Just think, Ross, when we were growing up, if I hadn't gotten my heart broken every few months by some jerkface, you might never have discovered your songwriting talents.''

He smiled and serenaded, '''Without you…I might have been a plumber. Without you…my life could have been a bummer.''''

She picked up the tune—or lack of one. "'You could have been a crooner…like Frank or Bing or Goomer. Truthfully, that doesn't rhyme, but if it helps, I know the time.'"

He groaned. "That's the reason I wrote the lyrics and you didn't."

"I just have to think about it longer, that's all. And your lyrics aren't all that terrific, you know."

"Which is why I became a doctor. Singing in the operating room doesn't garner that many critics."

"Remember the time you were going to drop out of ninth grade and take Nashville by storm?" Ellie's lips curved with the memory of those long-ago dreams. "I was going to go with you, and we were both going to get jobs on Music Row until you got discovered."

"That's right." He was quiet for a minute, remembering. "Now why would you have gone with me? You were never interested in being a star."

She shrugged easily. "It was the adventure. The idea of living somewhere other than here. I guess it never occurred to me I could do something like that without you."

"There have been moments when I wished

you'd gone with me to Northwestern and even on to medical school, too.''

"I'd have gone in a heartbeat, you know that. But I thought a big university like that was way beyond my reach. Even with scholarships and loans, Mom would have worried herself sick about the money and me being so far away. She needed me to stay close and Uncle Owen wanted me to have the garage and… Well, I'm a small-town girl, Ross. The dreams I had were good ones, but the dreams I have now are just as grand, just as good.''

She felt the question in his gaze as it turned to her. "And these dreams…the ones you have now…why don't I know about them? Best friends share their dreams, you know. It's part of the pact.''

"They're the same ones I always had, Ross, just in a little different form. I want satisfying work to do, which believe it or not, I've found as a mechanic. I like working on cars and I like doing it in Bachelor Falls. Someday I want a home of my own, a husband, children, to live and love and know that I matter to the people who matter to me. Not as grand as going to Nashville or having an MD after my name, maybe, but it doesn't feel as if I settled for less. It feels…right.''

Silence settled between them like a kitten, soaking up the warmth of a sunny afternoon...and that, too, felt right.

A few miles down the road, Ellie quietly asked, "Does Tori know you once dreamed of writing poetry and song lyrics, Ross?"

"The subject hasn't come up." He kept his eyes on the highway, his hands on the wheel.

Ellie knew the subject would never come up. Tori saw Ross the way she wanted to see him, the way his parents had always seen him, the way he thought he was supposed to want to be. Oh, becoming a doctor fulfilled some of his own ambitions, Ellie knew, but she also understood that it hadn't been his idea. At least, not in the beginning. He hadn't wanted to go that far away to school or to spend so many years in the pursuit of a medical degree. The night before he left for Northwestern for his freshman year at college, he'd come to Ellie, all set to run as far and fast as he could. To Nashville or New York or the Caribbean. To a life where the expectations were his own and not anyone else's. Ellie had talked him into going to school, to do the thing she felt he really wanted to do, anyway. She'd sometimes wondered if she had done the right thing.

"Do you remember the song you wrote for

graduation, the one about seeking life and finding love and daring to be brave?''

"That was such a long time ago, Ellie. I've forgotten most of it. It's written down somewhere, I just don't know where.''

"That's okay. I know it by heart…in case you ever need to recall all those wild, young dreams.''

He looked at her…and smiled a soft and sentimental smile. ''If I ever need to remember, I'll let you know.''

She nodded and gave him her best and brightest grin. ''And if I ever want to blackmail you, there's always this—'Belinda…my heart is yours, Belinda. Your eyes of blue, your hair of gold, your lips are like the sweetest rose. Paradise is in your smile. For your kiss, I'd walk ten thousand—'''

"I must have written at least a hundred dumb songs and that's the only part you remember?''

"Oh, no. I remember a bunch of them. Which one do you want to hear? Let's see, there was 'Beth, Beth, her name is Beth. The love of my life…her name is Beth.' And then there's another of my particular favorites, 'Debbi, do…oh, Debbi, please. Debbi, babe, I'm on my knees.'''

His cringe made her effort worthwhile. ''Those

are just the highlights," she said. "I can sing the whole song, if you want."

"If I thought I could stand it, I'd insist that you sing every verse of every song stuck in the crevices of your rotten brain. But it would be torture for both of us, so... 'Ellie, don't. Please, Ellie, don't. Ellie, babe, I'm on my knees, don't extend my agony!'''

They were both still laughing when steam began to boil up from beneath the hood and the BMW cruised to an overheated stop at the side of the road, twenty miles out of town.

Chapter Seven

The town hall was festive with green and yellow decorations...green on one side of the community room and yellow on the other. The bridal shower committee had obviously had a small disagreement. When Ellie and Ross walked in at seven-forty, a little the worse for their car trouble, the surprise was over and the wedding shower was already in progress. Bachelor Falls had turned out in force to get a good, long look at Ross's bride-to-be and, at the front of the room, surrounded by silver, white and pastel packages, Tori sat in happy, center-of-attention splendor, the empty chair beside her covered with swatches of torn wrapping paper.

"Ross!" She waved gaily the moment she saw him and heads turned to peruse the appearance of the late arrivals. "You missed the surprise."

"Car trouble." Ross answered the question inherent in every raised eyebrow and curious expression. "Busted water hose."

"Oh." It was a collective understanding that had heads nodding across the room.

Tori's laugh carried above the other noise, playing to the crowd. "Good thing he had his mechanic with him, isn't it, folks?"

Beside him, Ross felt Ellie stiffen and was torn between wishing Tori hadn't made it sound so servile and knowing she didn't understand the first thing about cars and what made them go. Or not go. "We had to call Chip to come out and tow us in, but here we are. Have I missed much?"

"Couldn't Ellie fix the car?" Tori asked. "I thought she could fix anything on wheels."

Ross pursed his lips, wanting to tell his beloved to drop the subject, even though he was sure she hadn't meant to sound catty. He moved away from Ellie and down the aisle between the rows of occupied chairs, shaking a hand here and there, stopping to say hi to this one and that one. As he reached the front, Tori stepped around the paper and packages to throw herself into his arms and kiss him soundly on the mouth. For the first time, Ross had no inclination to kiss her back.

"What's this?" She pulled back and began patting the bulge in his shirt pocket. "Have you been shopping, Ross? Did you buy something for me?''

He didn't know if there was a rule of etiquette on the appropriate timing to hand over the bride's gift, but now suddenly seemed as good a time as any. Pulling the slender box from his pocket, he offered it to her. ''It's for you,'' he said with a rueful smile. ''A wedding gift from me to you.''

Tori's lips formed a cute pucker of surprise as she took the box and shook it lightly, again playing to his friends and neighbors. ''Can I open it now?''

''I don't know.'' Ross smiled down at her, but couldn't shake a feeling of complete ambivalence. ''Can you?''

She pouted prettily and tapped his chin with her fingertip. ''Okay, smartie, *may* I open my present?''

''Open it!'' someone called from the back.

''Come on, Ross…let her open it now.'' Tommie Nell stopped fussing with the ice ring in its rubber heart mold long enough to second the motion.

''There seems to be a consensus,'' Tori said happily. ''So, I guess I'll open it now.'' She slipped a fingernail beneath the silver ribbon and slid the bow to one side.

As she tore at the paper with undignified eagerness, Ross looked for Ellie and saw her standing in the back, leaning against the wall. Aunt Ona Mae Hunyacre stood next to her on one side and Shorty leaned against the wall on her left. Ellie had taken off her ball cap before they came inside and he could see the red bill sticking out of her overall side pocket. She hadn't rebraided her hair after the tuxedo fitting, but had pulled it back in a full, feathery ponytail that she'd then pulled through the sizing loop of the Cardinals cap. Now, without the ball cap to contain it, the ponytail spilled behind her shoulders, leaving curly tendrils to frame her face and ears. It was the way he often thought of Ellie…all eyes and hair and smile.

"Oh, Ross…" Tori's breath of delight brought his attention to her again, and he watched as she drew the bracelet from the box and across her wrist to show it off to the assembled audience. "Isn't it beautiful?" she crooned. "Oh, it's just perfect. Exactly what I would have chosen if I'd been with you."

He couldn't help it. He met Ellie's gaze and acknowledged the slight didn't-I-tell-you lift of her shoulders. "I'm glad you like it." He accepted Tori's thank-you kiss with the same antipathy as before, wondering vaguely if he'd have been happier if she hadn't liked the pearls. No one else seemed to notice his lack of enthusiasm, though, and applause broke out as the kiss came to an unexciting end. Tori blushed and tears of happiness glistened in her eyes, although Ross uncharitably thought it had more to do with the response of the Bachelor Falls populace than with him. Looking out at the familiar faces, the remembered smiles of his childhood, the fond and admiring expressions, he felt the tug of his roots and the knowledge that simply being born a Kilgannon made him a hero in their eyes. A hero, with all its attendant expectations.

Squaring his shoulders, he smiled back, deciding that if the people of Bachelor Falls wanted to give him this surprise wedding shower, the least he could do was enjoy their goodwill and good wishes. Rubbing his hands together in contrived anticipation, he looked around at the abundance of wrapped packages. "What can I open?"

"You *may* open any gift you like," Tori told him, sharing the little joke with everyone in an encompassing giggle. "Why don't you open that large package over there?"

"That's from me, Ross!" Ernie Potts pointed out his oversize gift from his third-row seat on the aisle. "I brought that big one," he said, proudly nudging Henry Boyd, who sat beside him. "It's a picture of the Grand Canyon."

Tori's bright smile dimmed a little as Ross peeled aside the wrapping paper to reveal that it was, indeed, a picture of the Grand Canyon. A very large picture. "Oh, thank you," Tori said graciously. "I know just where we'll put that."

Ross, not knowing what else to do, reached for another gift.

SOMEWHERE BETWEEN THE BMW's busted water hose and the moment Tommie Nell shoved a serving of carrot cake and store-bought mints into her hands, Ellie lost her appetite. If it hadn't seemed churlish and immature, she would have blamed it on Tori's lilting giggles and excited "Oh, thank you!" repeated again and again. Or on Ross's doting attentiveness to Tori's every word throughout the opening of the gifts. As it was, Ellie was stuck with no legitimate explanation for her nagging queasiness...except the two-inch thick cream-cheese icing on the carrot cake.

Before she could find a place to set the plate where she wouldn't have to see it, Mabel was taking it from her and substituting another, piled high with apple pie. "Here," Mabel whispered gruffly, looking around to see if anyone was watching. "I brought this from the diner. You'll like it much better than Hazel's dry old carrot cake." She scurried off, only to be followed a minute later by Hazel, who swapped Ellie's pie for another piece of cake.

"She's a crazy woman," Hazel whispered in

passing. "Thinkin' anybody wants her sour old apple pies. Can't give them away at the diner, that's why she's hustlin' pie over here." Shaking her head of gray-gold curls, she trotted off to get more cake to replace the cake Mabel was replacing with pie.

"They're both loonier than two ducks on a picnic," Aunt Ona Mae said...as if she had any room to talk. "I can outcook both of 'em with gloves on and wearin' bifocals."

Ellie smiled and nodded, which was always the best answer to practically anything Aunt Ona Mae said. "Do you want my piece of cake?" she offered.

The older woman sniffed. "I don't eat cake."

"You and Tori have a lot in common," Ellie commented dryly.

Aunt Ona Mae peered, squint-eyed, across the great hall at Tori and Ross, who were holding hands and laughing together with Tami and Travis, Bobby Joe and Carla. "Young people," she said, shaking her head. "Don't know what they have to cackle about. Just 'cause they decide to get married and people give 'em toasters and such things, don't mean life's a bed of dandelions."

Ellie looked around for diversion, and somewhere to put her cake plate.

"Know what *I* gave 'em?" Aunt Ona Mae

wasn't going to let Ellie escape just yet. "A bolt," she informed Ellie with a sage nod. "I stole it from the Bostian's space ship. Took it right off one of their light panels. It ought to be worth a lot of money once the government admits they've known about the aliens ever since Roswell."

Ellie was beginning to feel a bit desperate when Mabel came back with more pie. "Give me that." She snatched the cake plate out of Ellie's hands and slipped the pie plate in with precision. "Don't let that woman shove any more of her cake at you, you hear?" She started to walk off, but turned and shook a stern finger under Ellie's nose. "You eat every bite of that pie, too. You're lookin' a might peaked."

"You're looking way too sickly to eat that piece of pie," Ross said in her ear as he reached around from behind her and grasped the edge of her plate. "Give it to me, but whatever you do, don't turn around. I don't want Tori to see me stuffing Mabel's apple pie down my throat."

Ellie let go of the plate and felt better immediately. "You'd better be quick," she said softly over her shoulder. "She's already starting to look around. She could spot you any second."

"That's why I'm standing behind you. I'm using your body as a shield."

"Great," Ellie said with a sigh. "Just the way I've always fantasized my body being used."

Ross peeked around her. "Turn just a little to your left. There. That's great. And I told her you needed to talk to me about the BMW, so look serious." He swallowed a hunk of pie under the eagle eye of Aunt Ona Mae. "Hello, Auntie," he said. "Great shower, huh? Thanks for the bolt."

"It's a bolt from Bost," Ona Mae informed him tersely. "And metal from another planet won't be any use for holding together something that shouldn't have been put together in the first place, if you understand my meaning."

"I wouldn't dream of trying to use a bolt from Bost for anything practical, Aunt Ona Mae. Tori and I will prize it strictly as a conversation piece, I promise."

"Hmmph," she said. "You're a moron." Then she stalked off with her back as stiff and straight as a postcard.

"Hey, congratulations, Ross!" Ned Laney walked up, hand thrust forward.

Ross grabbed Ellie's arm and pulled it behind her back, where he ditched the empty plate into her outstretched fingers before reaching around her to accept Ned's felicitous pump of a hand-shake. "Thanks, Ned," he said. "And I can't wait to look over that book on horticulture. Great gift."

Ned flushed red with pleasure. "Thought you might find it interesting. Plants are our friends, you know."

"Ross, my man!" Another high school friend Brad Elston approached Ross from the other side and Ned backed away. "Let's get out to the lake and get in some fishing tomorrow. If the little woman will allow it, of course." Brad flirted with Ellie in a sideways glance. "You can come, too, Ellie. I'll let you...*bait my hook.*"

Ellie gave him the benefit of her most sultry smile. "I never touch anything resembling a worm, you know that, Brad."

He clutched his chest. "You're breakin' my heart, Ellie," he said to her, then complained to Ross. "She's always like this with me. Cold and cruel. But I think it's because she's secretly in love with me. She's just hiding her true feelings beneath a facade of dislike. That's it, isn't it, Ellie?"

She upped the wattage of the smile. Brad was handsome and shallow, but as long as they stayed away from real conversation, she sort of enjoyed flirting with him. "You've guessed my guilty little secret, Brad," she said. "I pine for you in private."

He waggled evil eyebrows. "My *privates* pine for you, too, sugar."

Ross nudged Ellie subtly but firmly out of the

way. "Isn't that Belinda Morgan waving at you, Brad?" He pointed a stern finger at Belinda and when Brad turned around, Ross waved enthusiastically at Belinda, who blinked, then waved enthusiastically back.

"Oh, hell." Brad's suave manner deserted him. "I've got to leave now before she gets over here. I'll see *you* tomorrow." He tapped the tip of Ellie's nose and scooted out the door.

"You're *not* going to see him tomorrow," Ross said, then asked, "are you?"

"As a matter of fact, I am."

"I thought we were going to work on my car."

She pursed her lips, a little surprised at the edge in his voice. "That won't take all day, Ross. A couple of hours, tops."

"But you said we'd have to drive over to Springfield again to pick up the new hose."

"Chip will get it." She looked at him. "I know how to handle Brad, if that's what's bothering you."

"Nothing's bothering me." He crossed his arms across his chest, as if that proved it.

"Good." She crossed her arms, too, just to be in sync.

"He tapped your nose," Ross pointed out, sounding a little insulted. "You don't like that, remember?"

"No. I just don't like for *you* to do it." She

handed off the plate to him just as Hazel darted up, two steps ahead of Mabel. "Have some cake," Hazel said, smoothly exchanging the empty plate for one brimming with cake.

"Wow, this looks good," Ross said.

"Give me that!" Mabel grabbed for the plate and came up with a handful of cake and icing.

"Food fight!" someone yelled...and Ellie made good her escape before the crumbs started to fly.

"WHERE DID YOU GET TO last night?" Ross leaned against the front fender of his BMW while Ellie worked at replacing the radiator hose. "One minute you were my shield and the next minute I couldn't find you anywhere."

"I slipped out before Mabel crammed carrot cake up Hazel's nose."

"That isn't what happened. You should have stuck around."

Ellie let her gaze slide to him from under the hood of the car. "Hazel smeared apple pie all through Mabel's new perm?"

"No, Belinda jogged up to say hi to me just as Mabel flung her hand to dislodge the cake which, unfortunately put her—Belinda, that is— in the direct line of fire."

"So Belinda got a face full of carrot cake?"

"Actually it hit her a little lower than the face.

On her chest, to be exact, and it sort of just... slid...down the front of her blouse."

Ellie could well imagine the scene that had created. "Let me guess. Every gentleman in the room stepped forward to unselfishly offer to help her get the cake out of her cleavage."

"Not *every* gentleman rushed to help. Someone had to protect what was left of the apple pies and carrot cakes."

Ellie matched his sudden grin. "So how much sugar did you put away during the brouhaha?"

He tapped his thumbs against his cheeks. "Enough to put these roses in my cheeks."

"And where was Tori during all this?"

"Guarding the gifts."

"Why? Did she think someone might steal them?"

He waggled a finger at her. "You forget, we received a genuine Bostian bolt. For all Tori knew, the government could have sent men in black to confiscate the alien material. There are conspiracies everywhere, you know. A giant cover-up."

"You're such a *cutup,* Ross," she said, mimicking Tori's giggly voice. "Either that or you have too much time on your hands. Get me the channel-lock pliers from the tool chest, will you?"

He returned a minute later. "Where's your watch?" he asked as he handed her the tool.

"I left it in the office. Why?"

"Just wondering when the last time was that you were thinking about me." He leaned his hips against the grill and crossed his arms. "Want to go fishing when you get through here?"

"Can't."

"You're going to close the garage for the rest of the week, anyway. Why not go ahead and do it a few hours early? Hours you can spend with me."

"We're closing at noon. I've already sent Chip home."

"Great. Then there's no reason we can't go fishing."

"I have other plans," she said, squeezing the clamp with the pliers as she maneuvered the ends of the hose into place. "Maybe Tori can find time to go with you."

"She's on her way to the airport to pick up Chrissy right now." He scuffed at a spot on the concrete floor with the toe of his loafers. "Why can't you go?"

Ellie concentrated on the tricky business of keeping the clamp open and her mouth shut. She'd promised Brad and the other guys that their plans for the afternoon would stay a secret. But keeping secrets from Ross was even harder than she'd remembered. "I have things to do," she said noncommittally.

"What things? I'll help you."

"You can't," she said quickly. "It's, uh, girl stuff."

"*Girl* stuff? What in the hell would that be?"

She rested her arms against the grill and frowned up at him. "You know what it is, Ross. Stuff that's of interest mainly to females. Surely Tori *occasionally* does things that are of absolutely no interest to you. That's girl stuff."

"I know what it is when Tori does it. I'm just having a hard time thinking of something you might do that would be of absolutely no interest to me."

"How about washing my panty hose?"

"You don't wear panty hose."

"How would you know? You've never once noticed what I was or wasn't wearing."

He grinned. "If you weren't wearing anything, I'd have noticed."

"Sure, you would." She turned her attention back to the radiator hose.

"So you won't go fishing with me because I've never cared whether you were naked or not?"

It was getting easier to keep the secret, Ellie decided. "Nope. I won't go fishing with you because I have other things to do. By myself." She handed him the channel-locks. "Put those away, would you, please?"

He did, turning back to her with a frown. "Hey, okay. I can take a hint. And I do have other friends, you know. One of them will want to go fishing."

"Good." She straightened and released the bar that kept the hood open. "Don't let me keep you, then. I'm sure there are fish out there trembling in their fins already."

"Okay," he said again. "Okay. I'll just take my car and go fishing."

She let the hood close with a solid, metallic thud. "You could always drive the Miata out to the lake. That would give the fish one last good laugh before they wind up in your frying pan."

He looked at her, his expression vaguely suspicious, his lips set in a thoughtful line. "What are you up to, Eliot?"

With supreme effort, she mastered the impulse to confess. "Girl stuff," she said, wiping her palms down the sides of her overalls. "Just as soon as you leave and I get cleaned up."

"Don't forget about the Miata. I drove it down here this morning so you could take a look at the transmission. Tori complains that it's hard to shift."

"She might try using the clutch."

He acknowledged her suggestion with a wry

smile. "Could you please take a look at it before you rush off to wash your panty hose? Tori took Mom's car to the airport, but she's planning to swing by here and pick up the Miata as soon as she and Chrissy get back to town. She wants you to meet Chrissy."

"Great," Ellie said dryly. "Can't wait."

"Serves you right," Ross said as he opened the door of the BMW and took the keys from his pocket. "You could have been fishing with me."

THE MIATA SHIFTED beautifully. Ellie couldn't find a single indication that it wasn't in perfect working order. But upon sliding the seat back so she could more easily get in and out, she made a very interesting discovery. Under the seat she found two Twinkie wrappers and a crumpled-up M&M's package. Plain. Not peanut. There was a trace of gooey filling left on one of the Twinkie wrappers and Ellie ran her fingertip across it out of curiosity. It felt sticky and reasonably fresh. A single M&M—a brown—rolled out when she uncrumpled the M&M's package and she held it in her palm for a minute, wondering. Then she broke it in half and popped one of the halves into her mouth, using her taste buds to determine if the candy was left over from Halloween or some other sweet-treat occasion. But the chocolate tasted as fresh as if it had gone from the assembly line to the store just yesterday.

"Now, what is this doing under your seat, Tori?" Ellie asked aloud and then smiled, feeling suddenly a little more optimistic about Ross's future.

"ELLIE? THIS IS Chrissy Kramer. Chrissy, this is T. S. Eliot." Tori's smile beamed from Ellie to Chrissy, her maid of honor. "She's not the real poet, though. She's just named after him."

Ellie glued on a smile and offered her hand to Tori's best friend in the world. "It's T. S. Eliot *Applegate*. I'm happy to meet you."

Chrissy, a full-figured, doe-eyed brunette, gave Ellie's outstretched hand a limp shake. "Me, too," she said, then giggled. "I mean, *you,* too. I'm happy to meet *you,* too."

"I couldn't wait to introduce you two." Tori clapped her hands with excitement. "Ross's best friend is here and my best friend is here and we're all together and now everything is just perfect."

"You don't look a thing like I thought you would," Chrissy said candidly. "Of course, I never met a woman mechanic before."

Ellie wanted to say she'd never met a nitwit's best friend before but decided *that* would have been mean-spirited. "We all look alike."

"Well, you're prettier than I expected," Chrissy went on. "Ross said you were attractive but, well, you know how men are. They don't always *mean* attractive when they *say* attractive. Sometimes it can sort of, well, have a different meaning altogether. If you get my drift…"

Ellie was pretty sure she got it. "I guess I should be grateful he didn't show you the picture of me and the Land Cruiser."

"The one where you've got all that mud in your hair?" Tori was obviously familiar with the picture. "You remember, Chrissy? Ross showed it to you that time at the country club. The snapshot of that awful old tank Ross used to love and Ellie? And they're both just covered with mud?"

"Ohh." Chrissy stretched the syllable while wrinkling her nose. "That was *you?* I thought it was some *guy.*"

Before the week was out, Ellie decided she was getting that picture away from Ross. "That was me," she said on a sigh. "Just one of the guys."

Chrissy's professionally arched, sixteenth-of-an-inch eyebrows went up. *"Ohhhhhh,"* she said.

"Noooooo." Tori frowned fiercely and shook her head. "She likes *boys.* Ross told me there's never been any…well, you know." She smiled

brightly at Ellie while correcting Chrissy's mis-conception. "Ellie is just a tomboy, that's all."

"Probably comes from being named after a man." Chrissy, too, smiled brightly, obviously feeling more comfortable now that she'd been re-assured as to Ellie's sexual preference. "I'd never do that to my little girl when I have one."

"Of course you wouldn't," Ellie said, pre-tending the tension in her jaw was just part of her own brilliant smile.

"But you know," Chrissy continued, "there was that country music singer who had a guy's name."

Tori frowned at her best friend. "I don't re-member that. Are you sure?"

Chrissy snapped her fingers, as if her memory was somehow attached to the action. "You know. She plays the guitar and has long hair and she used to sing with her mother...."

"The Judds?" Tori asked.

"That's it." Chrissy nodded, happy to have that mystery solved. "Judd. And being named after a man hasn't ruined her life."

"That's her last name." Tori gave Ellie a pay-no-attention-to-her look. "And it's just a stage name, too. Wynonna and Naomi Judd. Wynonna has a solo career, now."

"*Whynonna?*" Chrissy repeated, wrinkling her nose. "Well, if I was going to have a stage name, I'd pick something pretty like Crystal or Chantel. Just the one name, like that. You know, Tori, like when you were going to be a singer, you wanted to be known as just *Tori!*''

It was Ellie's turn to raise her eyebrows, even though they hadn't been professionally plucked. ''You were going to be a singer?''

Tori blushed. ''Oh, that was a long time ago.'' She glanced at her dainty gold watch. ''We *have* to go, Chrissy. Thanks for looking at my car, Ellie. Guess we'll see you Thursday night at the rehearsal if not sooner.'' Pushing a set of car keys into Chrissy's hand, Tori opened the office door and stepped outside. ''Come on, Chrissy. Bye, Ellie!''

Chrissy looked surprised by the sudden hurry, but she told Ellie goodbye as Tori all but jerked her through the doorway and out to the car. Odd, Ellie thought as she watched them leave. Twinkies and *Tori!*

Ross loved sweets, but not Twinkies. Tori abhorred sweets, but there were incriminating Twinkie wrappers in her car. Ross had once dreamed of being a songwriter and Tori had once harbored hopes of being a country-western singer. Maybe the two of them had more in common than she'd first thought. Ellie found the idea totally depressing.

Either that or her mother had ruined her life by naming her after a man.

Chapter Eight

Thick, gray clouds edged the afternoon in an early dusk and Ellie finished packing the El Camino with one eye on the sky and one on the clock. But by six, when the camping gear was loaded, tied down and covered with a tarp, the clouds had moved on. Now all she had left to do was find Ross and get him up to the falls so the bachelor shower could begin.

She found him alone in the last place she'd thought to look...at his favorite fishing spot a half mile downstream from the falls. He was standing in the deepest part of the stream, with water swirling nearly to the top of his hip boots, fly casting into the shade along the far bank. She picked her way down the grassy slope. "Having any luck?"

He pulled the rod back to the two-o'clock position, then cast forward to the ten, sending the line spiraling across the water. "I thought you were busy doing girl stuff."

"I was," she said, watching the smooth, even rhythm of his body as he yanked the line up and cast again. "I spent the afternoon getting ready for a hot date."

His gaze flicked over her faded blue jeans, navy striped T-shirt and red Cardinals ball cap. "Can't be too hot. You're not wearing panty hose."

"They'd just be in the way."

There was a slight hitch in his cast and the lure fell into a swirl of sunlit water. He pulled it back and started over, this time sending the line unerringly into the deep shadows along the bank.

Ellie smiled to herself. "Are they biting?"

"Not at the moment."

"It's too late in the day for trout," she pointed out. "Unless you're hoping to wake one up."

"I'm not fishing for trout." He sent the line soaring out across the stream once again. "I'm thinking."

"What about?"

"Guy stuff."

"*Mmm.* That would be the stuff guys think about when women aren't around, I suppose."

"That would be it, yeah."

"Couldn't find anyone to come fishing with you?"

"I didn't ask anyone else. I decided if you didn't want to spend the afternoon with me, I'd just as soon be by myself."

Ellie stuck her hands into the hip pockets of her blue jeans and watched him cast twice... three...four times before she spoke again. "Must be kind of scary being this close to a lifetime commitment," she said. "I'd probably want to think about it, too."

His gaze cut to hers, as fleeting as the lure's touch on the water. "Who said that's what I was thinking about?"

"No one. That's just what I'd be thinking about if it was only a couple of days before my wedding."

"For your information, I wasn't thinking about that at all." He cast a few more times in pensive silence. "I was thinking that if I left now, I could be fishing for Alaskan salmon by this time Saturday."

"Or you could be on a fishing boat off the coast of Florida, angling for marlin."

"Or I could be waiting tables in Nashville, hawking song lyrics to every aspiring singer who comes in." His smile was part regret, part resignation, all wry self-directed humor.

"But you're not leaving," she said.

"No, I'm not leaving." He began wading toward the bank, reeling in the line as he moved against the flow of the stream. "I'm going to get out of these boots and go home to my fiancée."

Ellie pursed her lips. "Actually, you're not going to do that either."

"I'm not?"

"No. You're coming with me."

"I really have no desire to wait tables in Nashville."

"Good, because that's not where I'm taking you."

He nodded, considering. "I'll need to call Tori, let her know how late I'll be getting back."

"I left her a note," Ellie told him.

"You left Tori a note," Ross repeated, his hip boots raining water as he trudged into the shallows and came out onto the rocky bank. "What did the note say?"

"'If you ever want to see Ross again, leave six hundred boxes of Twinkies in the trunk of your car. P.S. This is a joke. We've just taken him camping.'"

Ross laughed. "The Twinkies were a masterful touch, Eliot."

"Thanks. I rather liked that part myself. I'm sort of wishing I hadn't put in that part about it being a joke."

"She'd never be able to fit six hundred boxes into the Miata, even if there was the ghost of a chance she could bring herself to buy something so nonnutritious.''

"Hmm.'' Ellie thought of the mysterious Twinkies wrapper, but kept the discovery to herself. ''Looks like you won't be going home to your fiancée tonight, then. No ransom, no mercy. Now get out of those wet boots and let's go.''

''Wait a minute. You couldn't come fishing with me, but you expect me to go camping with you?''

She picked up his tackle box. ''You don't get a choice, Ross. As your best man, it's my duty to inform you that you are now officially kidnapped.''

''Hot damn. Tonight's my bachelor party.''

''Bachelor *shower,''* she corrected.

''What's the difference?''

''At a shower you get presents.''

He cocked his head, considering. ''And at a bachelor party…?''

''You don't.''

''Big difference,'' he said.

''I thought you'd see it my way.''

THIS WAS GOING TO BE great. Ross balanced a tin plate on his knees, picked up the hot dog he'd just roasted—his third—and bit into it with gusto. Next to him, Bobby Joe was eating pork and beans out of a can, and on the other side of him,

Travis was twisting the top off a Bud Light. Across the campfire, Ellie was roasting marshmallows on a stick. Shorty Silvers, Brad Elston and Ned Laney had gone down to the stream to do some "night fishing," they'd said, but in actuality to smoke the cigars Ross had seen Brad slip out of his backpack and into his pocket. There wasn't a detectable scent of tobacco in the cool spring night, just the pungent smell of burning hickory limbs. Occasionally a murmur of distant voices floated up from the bank below.

This was the life, Ross thought as he savored the slightly charred taste of the hot dog and the camaraderie of his friends. He remembered with clarity the last time he'd spent the night in these woods near the falls. It had been the late August night before he left for Chicago, college and the life he now lived...for better or worse.

"Hey, Ellie," Travis said. "Roast a marshmallow for me, would ya?"

"Sure." She swivelled the stick in her hand and a marshmallow slid off the end and into the fire. "There. Yours is roasted."

Bobby Joe laughed. "Good one, Ellie."

"Oh, yeah. Real funny," Travis said dryly. "Toss me that bag of marshmallows, Applegate."

"You're not getting the whole bag." She took

a single marshmallow from the bag and tossed it across the fire.

Travis caught it in one hand. "Can I borrow your roasting stick?"

"The Ozarks are full of tree limbs," came her answer. "Get up and get one."

"I gave you my hot dog," he protested. "The least you can do is let me borrow your hickory limb so I can roast one measly marshmallow."

"You only gave me the hot dog because you let it catch fire and it got a little burned."

"I don't eat burned wieners." Travis popped the whole marshmallow into his mouth and washed it down with a swig of beer. "A man has to have some standards. Ain't that right, Bobby Joe?"

Bobby Joe answered with a profound belch. "Damn straight. Men like us *live* by our standards."

Ross took another bite of his hot dog, in no hurry to be asked his opinion on standards. Ellie smiled as she caught his eye through the shimmer of heat waves above the fire and he smiled back. Yes, he thought. This was the perfect bachelor party. Shower. Bachelor shower. There was a suspicious-looking lump covered by an orange tarp sitting between the two large three-man tents. Ellie's small, one-man tent was pitched farther left, a discrete distance from the other two—the only deference paid to the fact that she wasn't one of the guys. Ross supposed the tarp covered his bachelor presents. No telling what embarrassments lay ahead of him tonight, considering his friends and the *standards* they lived by. He just hoped Ellie's presence would mute what could otherwise be a raucous and randy gift-giving. Although why he even gave it a thought was a mystery. Ellie had proven through the worst of hormone-laden adolescence that she could handle these males. Hell, she could probably handle these and a dozen more and never even break a sweat. It had been a long time since she'd needed a bodyguard...if she'd ever really needed one at all.

The cigar smokers returned to the campsite, sans the cigars, but bringing the faint odor of tobacco back with them. Shorty squatted down next to the fire, midway between Travis and Ellie. Ned turned a bedroll on end and sat on it, balancing his weight with the balls of his feet, his knees jacked upward in a sharp, roller-coaster angle. Brad circled the group like a hungry wolf and dropped to the ground next to Ellie. Close to Ellie, Ross noticed. Nearly in her lap.

"So what do we do now, Ellie?" Ned asked.

"Yeah," Travis seconded the question. "This is the first time I've been out this late without

Tami since I got married. I'm not going to bed down before midnight.''

"Yeah," Shorty said with a yawn. "What did we do at your bachelor party, Bobby Joe?"

"We got tanked."

"What about yours, Travis?"

"Drunk as toads in a huddle."

Ned frowned. "Well, what about Harlen Daniels's bachelor party? He doesn't drink."

"Since when?" Brad asked, sprawling on his side, which, Ross noticed, put his head almost in Ellie's lap.

"Since he got engaged to Reverend Minks's daughter Georgia," Bobby Joe answered. "And at his bachelor party we sat around and told dirty jokes until we passed out from boredom."

"What are bachelor parties like in Chicago, Ross?" Shorty wanted to know. "You must have been to a few."

"Drinking and dirty jokes there, too," he said with a shrug. "A lack of imagination must be pretty universal."

"I thought every bachelor party had to have a stripper." Ellie looked expectantly around the group as she licked the marshmallow stickiness off her fingers.

"You volunteering?" Brad grinned up at her and Ross wondered if he really thought that was funny. It was pretty obvious no one was laughing. But with a glance at the faces lit by the fire's glow, Ross realized no one had taken the idea seriously, either. The other men were all grinning, too, waiting to see how Ellie would put Brad in his place.

She took her time, sucking the last bit of sticky sweetness off the pad of her thumb...and looking sexier than Ross had ever imagined she could. And suddenly he couldn't stand to sit there a minute longer and watch Brad Elston ogle her as if he wanted to put her fingers in his mouth and suck—

Ross practically jumped to his feet, sending his plate and half-eaten hot dog skittering along the edge of the fire. "Let's go swimming," he said. "I think we need to cool off a little."

Six pair of eyes turned on him with startled precision. Twelve eyebrows lifted in nearly simultaneous question. "Swimming?" Ned repeated. "Now?"

"Yes, now," Ross said, feeling foolish, but still determined to get Brad away from Ellie and maybe drown him. "Come on, let's go."

"Sit down, Ross. It's too cool to swim." Ellie's frown made little lines around her full and sensual mouth. "You'll catch pneumonia and Tori will never forgive me."

"We've gone swimming in temperature's half again as low as this," he stated stubbornly. "And my health really doesn't fall under the best man's job description, does it?''

The tension crackled like the green hickory limbs in the fire. Everyone looked uncomfortable as he and Ellie stared at each other across the campsite. Then, with a shrug, he played a strictly male trump card. ''You guys aren't *chicken,* are you?''

''Damn it, Ross.'' Travis pushed reluctantly to his feet. ''I didn't even bring my swimsuit.''

''Since when has that ever stopped you?'' Bobby Joe laughed as he, too, got to his feet. ''Ellie's the only one of us who doesn't go skinny-dipping.''

''More's the pity,'' Brad said, and Ross couldn't wait to get him into the water.

''If it wasn't your last camp-out as a bachelor, Ross, you could go swimmin' without me.'' Shorty unfolded like a carpenter's ruler and slapped a streak of dirt off his pant leg. On his way up, Ned picked up the bedroll and tossed it toward the tent.

The grumbling continued, but good-naturedly now, and Ross began to feel better. Until he glanced expectantly at Brad, who hadn't made any move to get up. ''Let's go, Elston,'' he said pointedly.

''You guys go on.'' Brad swung his body into an upright position, bringing his shoulder flush against Ellie's. "I try to stay out of cold water on nights like this."

"Nights like what?" Travis pulled his shirt up over his head and Ross came very close to asking him why he was doing so in front of Ellie. But they'd all been bare-chested in front of her at one time or another. Ross included. It just had never bothered him before.

"Yeah," Shorty asked. "What's so special about this night?"

Brad grinned, his lascivious gaze sliding to Ellie. "I think this is going to be my lucky night and I sure don't want to be *Chicken Little.*"

Ross's jaw clenched, but Ellie just laughed. "As opposed to other nights when you're just a chicken?" she said.

Bobby Joe, Ned, Shorty and Travis all burst out laughing. "You asked for that, Brad," Travis finally said. "Now are you coming with us or staying here so Ellie can humiliate you in private?"

Brad shrugged complacently. "I'll stay. She only abuses me because she loves me. Isn't that right, sweetcakes?"

Drowning was too good for the son of a—

"Ross?" Bobby Joe grabbed his arm. "You started this, now get the flashlight and lead the way. We're going swimmin'!"

Ross scowled one last time across the campfire, but Brad didn't move and Ellie didn't tell him to and there really wasn't anything else to be done. Except lead the troops to the swimming hole, leaving Ellie alone with Turkey Lurkey. "Who needs a flashlight," he said tersely. "Real men navigate by the stars."

BRAD'S CONVERSATION WAS pretty well limited to three topics: sports, life insurance, which he sold, and sexual innuendo. Ellie had exhausted the subjects of sports, term and whole-life policies, and was just about to switch to a philosophical discussion, which she hoped would put him right to sleep, when Ross and the others returned. Their deep-chested laughs rose up the bank ahead of them and, with a sigh of relief, she got to her feet to greet them. Snow White welcoming home the seven dwarfs. Except there were only five of them and she was a long-distance throw from being Snow White.

Ross was the first one to emerge from the darkness and he strode toward her, solemn and purposeful. The dying fire sent up a shower of sparks that burnished streaks of gold in his wet dark hair. He missed a step when he saw her, but not so anyone would notice. Except she noticed. She didn't know what was wrong with him all of a sudden, wasn't sure she wanted to know. Whatever he had on his mind, though, hadn't been soothed by a swim in the cool waters below the falls. She could see the tension in the set of his shoulders, the tightness along his jaw, the accusing expression in his eyes.

Accusing? Ellie pondered that impression as the other men reclaimed their places around the campfire. "Whew!" Shorty ran a long hand across his crew cut. "That was great! You guys shoulda been there."

"We were busy," Brad said as if he had something to brag about. "Ellie didn't want to look at a bunch of limp...*chicks* when she could be alone with her hero."

Shorty looked all around. "You mean, Superman was here?"

"Yes," Brad said importantly. "You've uncovered my mild-mannered secret disguise. *I* am Superman."

Ned grinned. "You look more like The Joker to me."

"The Joker is Batman's nemesis, you goofball." Bobby Joe threw his balled-up socks, missing Ned by a yard. "Superman has to pit his wits against Lex Luthor."

"Well, Brad doesn't have any wits to pit," Shorty said. "So he can't be Lex Luthor."

"Wasn't he bald?"

"Who?"

Travis leaned across Shorty to grab the bag of

marshmallows. "Gene Hackman. He was Lex Luthor in the movie."

"I thought we were talking about Superman."

"*I* am Superman," Brad repeated. "Ask Ellie."

They all looked at her...except Ross. "He is Superman," she said. "In his own mind."

Laughter bounced, deep and male, around her.

"Floored you again, Elston." Travis popped a whole marshmallow into his mouth and talked around it. "Ellie's never going to give you the time of day."

"You guys are just jealous because she wanted to stay here with me instead of going skinny-dipping with a bunch of—"

"Limp chicks," Ned supplied flatly. "Yeah, you said that already. Tell us something we haven't heard before."

Brad patted Ellie's hand. "Don't worry, sugarbear. I would never tell these hayseeds what we've shared together. They have no concept of...*paradise.*"

"Give it up, Elston." Bobby Joe handed him a beer and Brad leaned forward to take it, moving his hand away from Ellie's before she could do it for him. "You wouldn't know what to do if Ellie ever looked at you any way but cross-eyed. Isn't that right?"

Ellie shook her head at their nonsense, noting

that Ross had not only not joined in the teasing, he hadn't come anywhere near a smile, either. If anything, he looked even grumpier than before. He couldn't think there was even a smidgen of truth in all of Brad's posturing. Ross knew better than anyone that she'd never been impressed with machismo and he had to know that if any man could change her mind, it wouldn't be Brad Elston. And yet there seemed to be a correlation between Brad's flirting and Ross's scowl. Either that or he was wishing Tori had come up with the Twinkie ransom.

Ned covered a yawn. "If you want me to be awake when you open your gifts, Ross, you'd better start now."

Travis chomped another marshmallow as he nodded agreement. "I don't know what's happened to me, but I can't stay up all night anymore like we used to."

"You got married and turned into a husband," Shorty said. "That's what happened."

"What did we tell you, Ross?" Bobby Joe said. "Marriage ruins a man's iron constitution. Why, these days I do good to stay awake past ten."

A wave of yawns—some real, some not—passed from one iron man to another. Bobby Joe finally got up and walked barefoot to the orange tarp. He handed the presents, one at a time, to

Brad, who passed them to Ellie, who sent them on around the circle to Ross.

"Open mine first," Brad said.

Ross picked up the paper bag just beside the envelope Brad had brought. "That's from me," said Ned. "It's a new reel for your fishin' rod."

"So it is." Lifting the reel from the sack, Ross held it up in the palm of his hand so everyone could see. "Thanks, Ned. I really appreciate having this. Can't wait to try it out."

Travis leaned over to pluck a flat package from the rest and toss it into Ross's lap. "Open that one. It's a tool."

It was a tool, a crescent wrench, wrapped in three pairs of jungle print briefs. Travis's face got red. "Tami did the wrapping. I told her not to put that underwear in there."

Ross tossed a pair back. "You keep those, Trav. Surprise Tami when you get home."

Bobby Joe guffawed. "She'd be surprised all right. Probably start calling him her little jungle kitty."

Travis threw the briefs, hitting Bobby Joe in the arm. "You wear 'em," he challenged. "See what Carla starts callin' you."

"I'll just do that." Bobby Joe folded the skimpy underwear and made a show of tucking it inside the waistband of his jeans. "I'll have her purring five minutes after I get home."

"Five minutes is a long time for you, Bobby Joe." Shorty and Ned laughed.

Travis reached over and snatched a second pair of jungle briefs from Ross's wrench. "Well, if Carla's gonna be purring, Tami will want to, too. Those two women tell each other everything."

Ellie smiled at their easy banter, still watching for the first signs of a silver lining in Ross's gloomy mood. Brad's gift—a fifteen-percent discount on a life insurance purchase—didn't make any improvement whatsoever. The collapsible pool cue, a joint gift from Shorty and Bobby Joe, brought a genuine smile, but it faded a little too quickly to be a real mood shift. Even the inflatable doll—a gift all the guys claimed to have brought, but that none of them would actually admit bringing—aroused only a couple of reluctant laughs from Ross. When the doll was put away, still in the packaging, Ellie raised up on her knees and dug deep into one pocket. Pulling out a set of keys, she threw them at Ross, who caught them on a reflex. "I couldn't wrap my gift in studly underwear and it's not anything you can blow up, but…congratulations, Ross. Be happy."

He looked at the keys and the Chevy emblem on the fob, and then his eyes found hers through the faint smoke wisping upward from the embers. "These are the keys to Hot Rod."

His voice broke slightly and Ellie had to swallow a knot of emotion in her own throat before she could answer. "You'll have to call her Rodette from now on, I guess."

"You can't give me your car, Ellie. You love it too much."

"Not that much," she lied. "And if love counts, she's always been half yours, anyway. I'm just giving you my half."

He shook his head, still clutching the keys as if they were a fragile flower he had to protect. "No, I can't accept this, Ellie."

"I've already signed over the title to you." She gave him her best and bravest smile. "Please, Ross. I want you to have it. I'll send Chip and Sarah to Springfield Friday morning to pick her up. It'll give him a thrill to get to drive a great car for a change."

He looked at her and swallowed hard. "Ellie, no. I love you for offering, but…"

"It's not an offer, Ross." She added a note of firmness. "It's a gift. Just say thank-you and shut up."

He didn't, couldn't, seem to say anything for a moment, but then Travis said, "Damn! I'll say thank-you. Give it to me." He made a grab for the keys, but Ross closed his fingers tightly around them.

"Thank you," he said. And then he shut up.

Chapter Nine

Ross couldn't sleep. The sleeping bag under him was lumpy and smelled as though it had been in someone's attic for twenty years…which maybe it had. Travis and Bobby Joe had been involved in a snore-off for the past couple of hours, their duet rising and falling in a sloughing cacophony. A storm was moving in from the west, and outside, the trees rustled with the advancing wind. In the tent, the air was stale and humid and heavy.

Rolling onto his back, Ross stared at the canvas above his head as it moved in, then out in response to the pull of the wind. Once, there had been nothing he loved more than sleeping outdoors. Once, the sounds of an approaching storm would have had his heart pounding with the anticipation of being out in its wildness. Once, these friends had comprised the only world he had ever imagined he would want.

The restlessness seized him and he lay there in the dark tent, wondering what was wrong. Pre-wedding jitters, he decided. It had to be that. He should have insisted the wedding be held in Chicago, among the people he and Tori worked with. But she was enamored of small towns, of this area of Missouri in particular. She wanted a wedding in a quaint little church, in a quaint little town, with her best friend and his best friend in attendance, and with all the people he so often talked about looking on. He'd filled her head with the characters and stories of his hometown and look where it had gotten him. Right back in Bachelor Falls with the friends he'd left behind.

Nostalgia. That was a part of this, too. Wanting to go back to a simpler time. Although it hadn't seemed simpler then. Funny that he still enjoyed the same things, that these friends still were the best he had, that his life away from Bachelor Falls was the one he dreaded going back to. In his heart of hearts, he knew this strange little town, in this beautiful area of the Ozark Mountains, would always be the home he yearned to return to. For a moment he imagined himself taking over Doc Spivey's clinic and taking care of colds, flu, broken bones, rheumatism and whatever else might beset the residents of Bachelor Falls. He and Tori would buy one of the old Victorian houses on Main Street, raise a couple of rowdy kids and he'd drive around town in the '57 Chevy convertible Ellie had given him for a wedding present.

The image faded as the canvas flapped vigorously over his head. It could never happen, he realized. Tori had their future planned. A house near her parents, dual careers until the first baby arrived, a luxury car for him, a sports car for her...until their growing family required a van. He would play golf on Thursday afternoons. She would join the junior league. And until he'd come home to get married, all her plans had seemed wonderful and worthy and something to cherish.

He had prewedding jitters. That was the only explanation.

Outside, he heard the crunch of a broken twig underfoot and a hushed conversation. He sat up, straining to make sense of the low murmur that floated in random syllables into his tent. Then he heard laughter and a cautioning *"Ssshhh!"* and knew one of the voices was Ellie's. What was she doing? Who was she talking to? It was already starting to rain. There was the occasional *plop* of a raindrop on the canvas and any minute the storm could begin in earnest. Surely she wasn't outside with Elston. She had more sense than to meet him outside with a storm coming.

Ross frowned, vaguely aware of the fluxing

beat of his pulse, vaguely conscious of an increasingly restless energy. So what was going on out there? Or *in* there? What if Elston had slipped out of his tent and into hers? What if they were together? In Ellie's tent. Just Elston and Ellie. Pushing at the folds of the sleeping bag, he jerked himself free, pulled on the jeans and shirt he'd taken off before bedding down, and moved to release the tent flap. The wind caught him full in the face, not strong enough to take his breath, but carrying a warning of imminent downpour. He scanned the campsite and saw only the tents and the moving shadows of the tree branches. The flap of Ellie's tent was unsecured, blowing loose. So was the flap of the other three-man tent, the one Brad Elston was sharing with Ned and Shorty. His gaze snapped back to the smaller tent.

Ellie was in there with Brad. Ross knew it, felt the jolt of knowledge deep in his bones. She ought to know better. *Did* know better than to get mixed up with a loser like Brad. But what if Brad had slipped into her tent uninvited? What if she needed help to get rid of him? What if...? Ross crossed the campsite in four long strides, stepping over what remained of the fire, and ducking down to push aside the flap and peer inside Ellie's tent. It was dark, and he sensed rather than saw her startled movement as she sat straight up. *"Ross?"* she whispered hoarsely.

He sank back on his heels and held the flap higher so he could see if there was a second shape occupying her sleeping bag. "Where's Elston?"

"What?" She leaned forward, bringing her face out of the deepest shadows of the tent. "He was with me a few minutes ago. We both got up at the same time, and... Why? Has something happened to him? Is he hurt?"

"Not yet," Ross said, realizing with a razor-edged anger that he'd been right. Elston had been here. With Ellie. "He was here, though? With you?"

"Yes. I told you that already."

"Is he coming back?"

"I certainly hope so. He couldn't have gone very..." Her whisper stopped. "What's happened to him, Ross? What's wrong?"

Ross didn't recognize the hot, hammering pulse-beat that rose like a tidal wave of disaster in his veins. He simply felt it sweep through him, a thing apart, a force he hadn't the means or the will to control. "You could have told me, Ellie, instead of letting me find out like this."

"Find out what?"

The defensive note in her voice pushed him on to indiscretion. "You could have told me you were sleeping with Elston. Then I would have known not to act like your outraged big brother when he was making his stupid Chicken Little remarks, when he was intimating that the two of you were *paradise* on wheels together.''

''What?'' The word cracked in the stillness. And then she was grabbing his arm and jerking him inside the tent with her, pulling the flap in after him and securing it to stop its irritating motion. ''What in the hell are you talking about, Ross?''

It was claustrophobic inside the small tent and all he could see in front of him was the dark shape that was Ellie. All he could hear was the quick in and out of her breathing. All he could smell was her smell. Her annoyance was like another presence, like an uninvited guest for dinner. Outside, the rain began and pelted the canvas walls surrounding them. Sense returned with the clarity of a cold shower. But it was a little too late to retreat quietly back to his own tent. Too late to stop this intrusion before it got started. Too late to analyze the emotion that had brought him here in the midst of this dark and stormy midnight.

''Ross,'' she repeated in a soft, threatening whisper. ''What is wrong with you?''

There was nothing for it but sheer, unadulterated brazenness. "Are you sleeping with Elston?"

"Brad?"

"Well, now we both know who we're talking about. *Are* you sleeping with him?"

"This is a joke, right? Brad put you up to this, didn't he?"

"Why would he do that? He, at least, must know if you're having sex with him."

"Sex?" Her voice rose, shrill above the sounds of the rain. "You think I'm having *sex?* In a *tent?* With all my *friends* sleeping not ten feet away? Is *that* what this is about? You're thinking *my* fantasy is to have *sex* with *Brad Elston* while camping out with *you* and four *other* males?"

"Keep your voice down," he cautioned. "Do you want them to hear you?"

"Oh, no," she said even louder. "I don't want them to *hear* me. I want them to *catch* me having *sex* with Brad. Oh, but *Brad* isn't here, is he, Ross? *You are!*"

She was losing it. Ross could tell. And just when he needed it most, his anger vanished. She wasn't sleeping with Brad. It had been stupid to even think… Maybe he'd been asleep and just dreamed this. Maybe he was going to wake up in his own sleeping bag and remember how mad she'd been in his dream and when he told her about it, they'd both laugh.

But he could hear the rain pounding down on her tent. He could feel her breath on his face, the agitated rise and fall of her breasts against his bare arm. If this was a dream, it was turning into a nightmare.

"Calm down," he said, though he knew immediately that was not what he should have said.

"Calm down," she repeated in a voice of deadly calm. "Calm down. You burst into my tent in the middle of a thunderstorm and accuse me of sleeping with one of my friends and I'm supposed to be *calm* and tell you that you're just mistaken?"

"I don't think *all* of our friends need to hear this."

"Oh, I don't see why not. If I have to defend myself—which, by the way, is not what I'm doing here—if I have to defend the perfectly legitimate privilege of sex between consenting adults—and I am old enough to consent, Ross—then maybe all of my friends need to hear this. Maybe I should write it up and get it printed in the Gazette for everyone to read—*Ellie Applegate is* not *having sex with her friend Brad Elston. Ellie Applegate is* not *having sex, period. Although she* could, *if she* wanted *to.*"

"Ellie—"

"And *if* she wanted to, it wouldn't be any of her *friends'* business! It wouldn't even be her *best* friend's business! It wouldn't be *anybody's* business, but hers and *whoever* she decided to have sex *with!*"

"Ellie—"

"Look, Ross, I can understand you being nervous and tense about getting married, but this is completely bizarre behavior. And you know what else? *It really isn't any of your business!*"

"Ellie—"

"You have nothing to say about whose sleeping bag I'm sleeping in. You have nothing to say about who gets to sleep in mine. Get it? It's none of your business if I'm hopping in and out of sleeping bags all over the country."

"Ellie—" He stopped, assuming she would interrupt him again, and when she didn't, it took him a second to realize he had the floor. "You're right. I'm sorry."

"You'd better be really, *really* sorry."

"I'm really, *really* sorry. I am."

"I cannot believe you thought—"

"I must have been having a nightmare or something." It was a cheap excuse, but the only one he thought she might find plausible. "I don't know what I was thinking."

"This isn't like you, Ross."

She was behaving a little strangely, too, he

thought. And she didn't even have prewedding jitters to blame. But pointing that out would probably not be the wisest response. "I know. I'm sorry."

"You've said that already."

"I know. I'm sorry." He *was* sorry he'd barged in on her like he had. But he wasn't sorry that she wasn't having sex with Brad. He was relieved. But saying he was sorry sounded better.

She was quiet for a moment and her anger began to feel more like a memory than a presence. "It really isn't any of your business, you know."

"I know." He reached for her hand in the dark, and found something else entirely.

"Ross," she said. "What are you doing?"

"I was looking for your hand...to give it a squeeze."

"That isn't my hand."

It was awfully close in here, he thought. Not much room at all. And there was warmth under his hand, and fuzz. Lots of fuzz. "What is it?"

"Purple Bunny."

"I'm squeezing Purple Bunny?" He pulled the rabbit toward him. "He's gotten fat, since the last time I squeezed him."

"I stuffed my jeans and T-shirt into that little pocket he has down his back. The one Lana and Kelly and I used to use to send notes to one another. Gives me a place to keep my clothes and makes a pretty good pillow for a camp-out.''

Ross's listening ability stumbled at the very beginning. ''If the rabbit is using your clothes for stuffing,'' he asked, because it seemed important for him to know, ''what are you wearing?''

''I travel light, but I never go anywhere without my Bachelor Daze Run The Gauntlet souvenir T-shirt. Can't sleep without it.''

He laughed softly, relaxing into the welcome darkness with its attending summer shower. Ellie always had this effect on him. No matter how angry they might get, or what bizarre things they said, it somehow always came out like this...with the gentle sharing of memories and the comforting knowledge that their friendship could survive anything. ''I suppose you're prepared to run tackle for me Friday at the forty-seventh running of the gauntlet.''

''You betcha. I've got my football padding and I'm set.'' She paused. ''But once we get to the falls, you're on your own. I'm not going to push you into the falls, Ross. I mean, I know that, as your best man, I'm supposed to try. And it's not like either one of us believes that it means anything if I did push you in. You'd still get married Saturday, regardless. But just in case there's any truth at all...''

''The Bachelor Daze race is just for fun, Ellie,

no matter how seriously some people may feel about it. But I'm giving you fair warning that you couldn't push me into the falls if you tried. You may have the edge when we play pool, but you are not going to be able to get me in the water come Friday.''

"Really?" She sounded interested in his little challenge. "Don't have a chance, huh?"

"Not even the glimmer of one." He could just make out the bobbing of her head in the dark. "So don't even think about it."

"Well, okay, if that's the way you feel——"

"That's the way I feel." He tried to shift positions in the cramped one-man quarters and bumped her shoulder hard. He caught her as she fell into the side of the tent and pulled her against him before she capsized and took their shelter down with her. Not that there had been much danger, but his reaction had been strictly reflex. Another reflex kicked in when she put her hands on his arms to right herself and her chin bumped his. Awareness clamped onto him with sudden, sure surprise and in a split second, he went from relaxed to aroused. *Wait a minute,* he told his over-eager body. *This is Ellie. My best friend.*

She thankfully didn't seem to notice anything remarkable about his stillness, didn't seem to know that there had been a shift in mood, however fleeting it might prove to be. "I'd better go,'' he said and was alarmed by the husk of desire he heard in his voice. *This is Ellie,* he repeated to himself. *Ellie. My best friend.* "I think the rain may be slacking off a little now," was what he said to her.

"You think so?" She tilted her head back to listen and his senses were filled with her scent and her hair—all that wild, fragrant hair, curled riotously, sensuously into his awareness. He had to get out of here. Now.

"Yeah." It was a desperate sound and he fumbled with the release of the tent flap, thinking a couple of minutes out in the rain would snap him out of this. A couple of minutes. That's all he needed.

"Ross?" Her voice stopped him.

This is Ellie. Just Ellie. He grasped control of his thoughts and held on to them. There was nothing wrong with him. Nothing. He was tense, stressed. He was getting married on Saturday. "Yeah?"

"I just wanted to tell you that no matter what stupid things you do, I still love you. As a friend."

"As a friend," he repeated, reminding himself of the same thing. They were friends. That was all. Except that he was behaving like an idiot. "Thanks, Ellie. Thanks a lot."

He didn't know she was going to hug him until

he felt her arms slide around his waist, until her hair brushed against his nose and mouth, teasing him with its fragrant summer sweetness. And he was positive she didn't know he was going to kiss her until the moment his lips closed over hers and the whole world turned upside down.

SOMEWHERE THERE WAS RAIN. A storm. Its energy was everywhere around her, surrounding her...in her. The thunder came from inside, pounding through her veins, roaring in her ears. Lightning heat seared her, consumed her, energized her...changed her. Ross's kiss was all she knew, the surprising claim of his lips held both discovery and denial. If she'd had any warning, maybe she would have turned her head at the crucial moment and never known the truth that now branded her with its veracity.

Ellie lifted her hand to Ross's face, felt the scratch of tomorrow's beard against her palm as their lips clung for a wondrous, torturous eternity. Then she somehow found the strength to pull away. But the storm didn't end. It lingered in the shaky breaths they each exhaled, in the hot, humid air surrounding them, in the weighty silence that said everything...and nothing. She trembled. Or maybe the whole world trembled.

Rain pounded down on the tent, its steady rhythms the only sound. Ellie wanted to scream into the silence, break it with her voice, shatter it with demands. She wanted to yell at Ross, berate him for being here, for kissing her, for stripping away the most precious illusion she had. She wanted to whisper to him that it was all right, that nothing had changed. She wanted to go back and turn her head, so she would miss his kiss, so she would miss the moment when her world shifted, spun around and brought her face-to-face with the realization that she was in love with her best friend.

"Ellie…?"

Her name was a throaty murmur in the darkness, but she couldn't answer. She didn't dare. She shook her head, pleading silently with him to go. Before the torrent of emotion broke free inside her and fatally wounded what was left of their friendship.

Whether Ross saw her movement or simply sensed that there was nothing to be said, Ellie didn't know. But she felt the air stir as he threw back the entrance flap and moved quickly away from her and into the downpour outside. A mist of rain…or longing…blew against her lips and she almost reached out to stop him. But she didn't. And he was gone. The tent flap dropped back into place, showering her with raindrops, closing her into darkness, into the terrible fear that she had just lost the best friend she'd ever have.

And then there was nothing but rain...in her ears...in her head...in her heart.

"WHAT HAPPENED to my socks?" Bobby Joe's voice woke Ellie from a deep, dreamless sleep and she sat straight up, bumping her head against the tent. A puddle of leftover raindrops ran from a shallow indentation in the canvas and splashed onto the ground next to the tent wall.

"Looks like you left 'em outside and they got soaked." Travis's answer held little sympathy. "Ruined 'em."

"Think the dirt would bleach out?"

"They're not worth that much effort, Bobby Joe. Throw them away." It was Ross's voice just outside her tent, and Ellie went still, remembering.

"Could dry 'em out and use 'em as rags."

"Ross is right. Throw 'em away." Travis said around a yawn. "What happened to everybody, anyway? I'm not usually the first one up."

"First one up, my ass," Bobby Joe said. "I was awake before you, and Ross was up before me. Look. He's already cookin' breakfast."

There was a clank of tin and utensils. "Don't even think of getting any closer to that pancake," Ross said in a firm but affectionate growl.

Ellie pulled her knees to her chest and stretched her Bachelor Daze Run The Gauntlet souvenir T-shirt down to her ankles. Ross had kissed her last night and there was no way she could go out there and face him.

"You know, we could get in a few hours of fishing before we have to go back," Travis said. "School's out for the summer and if I don't make the teacher's meeting this afternoon, no one's going to care. There ought to be some perks to being the high school principal."

"Yeah, but the question is…" Bobby Joe's voice was gruff with fun. "Do you have a note from Tami sayin' it's okay for you to go fishing?"

"I'll show you my note…if I can read your permission slip from Carla."

There was some scuffling and some laughter and when Bobby Joe spoke again, his voice was muffled, as if his back was turned. "I don't have to be home any time special. Carla and I closed the print shop for the rest of the week so we could enjoy the Bachelor Daze festivities. You want to go fishing, Ross?"

"Sure. That'll give me a chance to test out my new reel," Ross said, sounding completely normal. Maybe he *was* normal. Maybe *she* was crazy. Maybe he'd become a sleepwalker and had no memory whatsoever of what had happened.

"I might even have time to break in my new pool cue at Ernie's before the wedding rehearsal tonight."

Ellie rested her forehead on her knees. Tonight Ross was going to practise getting married. And she'd have to be there. The best man had to be there. She was going to be sick.

"How come these guys are sleeping so late?" Bobby Joe asked. "Let's wake 'em up."

"Yeah," Travis answered. "I know Ned brought a box of doughnuts, but I can't find them anywhere out here."

"He's probably sleepin' with them, so you can't have any." Bobby Joe's voice came nearer and then there was a *whump* on the canvas wall of her tent. "Hey! Applegate! Wake up in there. We need a *woman* to fix our breakfast! Get up and get your sleepy butt out here pronto!"

"Go away," she muttered. "You sadist."

"I heard that, Snow White. Now get up unless you want me and the seven dwarfs to start singin' falsetto."

"There's only six of you," she pointed out.

"I'll sing twice." Bobby Joe's footsteps moved on and Ellie reached for Purple Bunny. His pudgy body felt strange in her hands, but his one-eyed, flop-eared expression was achingly familiar. "I can't face him," she whispered to the rabbit, who had no answer. How could she face

Ross? Even if, by some miracle, she'd imagined the whole thing, she *knew*. And if she hadn't imagined the whole thing...well, then, *he* knew, too.

The *whump* came again, then Travis's voice. "Applegate? There are trout out there making fun of you. Get up! Let's go fishin'!"

"I hear you," she said roughly and knew she would have to get dressed and go out there and see Ross.

There was a series of muffled thumps from the other tent, followed by a trio of surprised yelps and a pithy string of curse words. "Hey!" Shorty's voice was loud. "What in the hell was *that* for?"

"Your morning shower," came Travis's laughing reply. "We just saved you three some time."

"We're goin' fishin'," Bobby Joe said with a laugh. "You were gonna get wet, anyway."

"You didn't have to get the tent all wet!" Brad sounded disgusted. "Damn it, Ramsey! Aren't you ever going to grow up?"

"Ah, Elston," Bobby Joe crooned. "Did we get your hair wet?"

"I'll get you for this."

"Ooh, we're scared, aren't we, Trav?"

"You're toast, Ramsey." Ned's voice joined the threat. "You, too, Ryals."

Ellie listened to the banter, heard the friendly scuffle, and told herself to get dressed before they came gunning for her.

ROSS WATCHED ELLIE'S TENT, waiting for her to come out, not knowing what to expect when she did. He should never have gone near her last night, should have minded his own business and stayed in his own tent. But that was water under the bridge now, and he had roughly five minutes to decide how to act when he saw her. If he behaved as if that midnight kiss hadn't happened, she might never speak to him again. On the other hand, if he made a big deal out of it, she'd know for sure that he was as insensitive as these other clods and she would definitely never speak to him again.

The worst part of it all was realizing that what he really wanted to do was to kiss her again. In the daylight. When he was thinking clearly. When no one else was anywhere near. When he could figure out if what he'd felt had been a fluke—or a fantasy.

"What is all the ruckus out here?" Ellie stepped out of the tent to face the day, and he stopped breathing. Her bright tones fooled him for a second. Her smile was wide and full of fun and, for an instant, he thought maybe he had dreamed that brief, soul-stirring kiss. But then her gaze collided with his and he knew that what had happened between them last night was even more serious than he'd allowed himself to believe.

"Ellie!" Travis drew her gaze and her attention. "Make Shorty leave me alone."

"You're paying for throwing water all over me," Shorty said, feinting an offensive move to the right, which sent Travis and Bobby Joe, who were facing the threat shoulder to shoulder, circling to the left.

"It was Bobby Joe." Travis stopped, hands out. "I was out here with Ross. Tell him, Ross."

"He was with me," Ross said, but the words sounded hollow in his ears. Not that these yahoos would notice. Not that he cared about anyone but Ellie at the moment.

"You want a piece of this, Kilgannon?" Ned asked, moving friendly-like from the other side of the campfire toward the culprits. "Because we can take you, too."

He wanted to talk to Ellie. Had to talk to her.

"Bobby Joe," Travis said while the two of them were backing away under the advance of the other three. "Waking them up was a really stupid idea."

"Yeah, wasn't it, though?"

Then the wake-ees made their move and all five men dashed like wild boys into the woods, leaving Ross a small but private window of opportunity.

"Good morning," he said over a lump in his throat that had to be as big as Wisconsin.

She looked at him and his heart hurt, and he was astonished to realize how great she looked fresh from sleep. He was even more astonished when he heard himself tell her so.

"Shut up, Ross," she said succinctly.

He did, for as long as it took to flip the pancake from the griddle onto a plate and offer it to her. "We need to talk," he said.

She shook her head, her eyes focused on the antics of the chase happening just beyond the clearing where they were camped. Her hair was tied in a loose knot at the back of her neck and the breeze lifted strands of her hair and blew them across her face. He wondered how he could have spent most of his life with her and never have seen her like this before. "What happened last night doesn't have to change anything, Eliot." He sounded desperate to convince her. He was desperate to convince himself. "But we have to talk about it. You know, clear the air."

Her gaze came back to him and he knew that he would do anything, say anything to keep her friendship. "There's nothing to talk about," she said, a coolness in her voice he'd never heard before. Not when she was speaking to him.

"You're tense. You're stressed. You're getting married on Saturday. And you're acting like a crazy person."

"Yes, but that doesn't excuse—"

"Yes," she said. "It does. It wipes it out. It didn't happen, understand? Talking about it is only going to make something out of nothing."

Not talking about it seemed to be accomplishing the same thing, he thought, but this was her call. It was becoming apparent that he wasn't going to get a vote. "So," he said to be sure he had his part straight, "I didn't go to your tent last night and we didn't ki—"

"That's right," she said so fast he knew that last night's kiss was going to be there between them from now on. The secret they pretended wasn't there. The one thing their friendship might not be able to survive.

Travis and Shorty ambled back into the clearing, laughing and looking none the worse for the morning's tussle. Behind them, Bobby Joe, Ned and Brad straggled in, still one-upping each other, still the same friends they'd been when the bachelor shower had begun. Only he and Ellie were different. Only he and Ellie had to pretend nothing had changed.

It would have been a hell of a lot easier to chase each other around the campsite, exchange a couple of not entirely friendly punches, wrestle a little, call each other names and come back still friends. It was the way guys settled things.

But as he was now very much aware, Ellie was *not* one of the guys.

Chapter Ten

"Ellie! Up here!" Tori called to her from the front of the church where the rehearsal was in progress. The entire wedding party was near the altar and, to a bridesmaid, they all turned to look back at the doorway where Ellie stood dreading the next couple of hours.

"Sorry, I'm late," Ellie called back. "Got stuck in traffic." It was a joke, but no one seemed to notice, so she put her reluctance in her pocket and walked down the aisle.

"You belong there beside Ross," Tori directed, motioning her to the dais where Ross stood, tall and unsmiling. "I put little pieces of tape down, see? That way you'll be in the exact, perfect spot."

"Perfect," Ellie mumbled as she stepped up to take her place on Ross's right. Well, it was his right side as long as he didn't turn around and look toward the back of the church which, of course, he would at the wedding when Tori made her entrance. Then Ellie would turn, too, and be on his left. And when he and Tori faced Reverend Minks, Ellie would be on his right again. Weddings shouldn't be confusing, she thought. And confused people shouldn't be participating in them.

"Ellie?"

She realized with a start that Reverend Minks was talking to her.

"Uh, yes?"

"You're on."

She wished she'd been paying attention. "On what?"

"No, no." The reverend shared his round-faced smile with the assembled parties. "It's your turn."

Was she supposed to turn? Was there something she was supposed to say? She looked to Ross for understanding, but he just stood there beside her, his hands clasped in front of him, looking at her with the same expectant expression as everyone else. "I didn't think I had to do anything but stand here," she said.

The bride and her bridesmaids giggled. "You have to keep my ring," Tori said. "That's the best man's duty."

Reverend Minks nodded a benevolent concurrence. "That's right, Ellie. At this point in the ceremony, I'll ask Ross if he has a ring for Tori as a token of his vows…like I just did. Then Ross will turn to you and ask for the ring…like he just did.''

''And unless you miss your cue, like *you* just did, everyone will live happily ever after,'' Chrissy said, and the bridesmaids giggled again.

Ellie forced her eyes back to Ross. ''Am I supposed to have Tori's ring?'' she asked.

He smiled, not a real smile, just a curving of the lips. She didn't think anyone would recognize that, though, except her. ''You're the official keeper of the wedding band,'' he said.

''Just Tori's,'' Chrissy was quick to add. ''I'm the keeper of Ross's wedding ring.''

Ross patted the pockets of his sports coat, then pulled out a diamond-studded band that could have blinded the entire wedding party if the light had struck it just so. ''Here.'' He held it out to Ellie. ''Now, you'll have the ring and when I ask you for it, you can hand it over.''

Tori gasped. So did Chrissy. So did the other two attendants, blondes with big, blue eyes. On Ellie's right, the other two groomsmen, Tori's male cousins from Milwaukee, blinked. As if to be sure *she* had the last gasp, Tori gasped again and covered her eyes. ''Ross! Put that back in your pocket and don't let me see it!''

"Don't let you see what?" Ross asked with a frown.

"The ring. The ring," Tori whispered from behind her fingers. "I shouldn't see my wedding ring before the ceremony."

"For Pete's sake, Tori. You picked it out. You've seen it a hundred times."

"But it's bad luck if I see it now."

"It's bad luck," Chrissy repeated ominously.

The bridesmaids nodded. The groomsmen blinked. Ellie wondered how much bad luck it would be if the ring accidently fell into the air vent under Ross's feet.

"You're supposed to keep my wedding band close to your heart until just before the wedding," Tori said.

"And if I don't, it's bad luck?" He sounded impatient, which Ellie thought was perfectly understandable.

"Bad luck," Chrissy agreed.

"Bad luck," Ross repeated with a weary sigh, his eyes finding Ellie's, his expression saying he'd had a run of bad luck already. Or maybe he was just tired. Tense. Stressed. Maybe that's all his expression was telling her.

He put the ring back in his pocket and his not-a-real smile moved to Tori, became real again. Soft, affectionate, bemused. Ellie thought she might be sick. "Tori," he said gently, as if she were a child who might not understand. "You know there can be no such thing as bad luck when it comes to you and me."

"Ohh." The bridesmaids sighed in unison, Tori uncovered her eyes and peeped up at him. And Ellie was sure she was going to throw up.

"Thank you," Tori said and patted his pocket, checking, Ellie supposed, to make sure the ring was actually back where it belonged. "You'll keep it next to your heart until Saturday?" Her smile flashed persuasively up at Ross. "Please? It will make me happy."

He tapped her cute button nose. "Your happiness is all I live for."

Ellie stuck her hands into her overall pockets and looked at the floor. She wasn't feeling sick anymore. Just miserable.

"Let's continue with the rehearsal, shall we?" Reverend Minks swept his hands through the air, his suggestion encompassing all participants and the observers—Tori's button-nosed parents, Ross's parents, Freda, Mrs. Minks, Mrs. Perkins and Melva Whiffington.

"Good idea," Ross said. "Let's wrap this up so we can eat."

"I'm hungry."

"Me, too."

The other two groomsmen showed some ani-

mation, and Ellie decided they weren't manne-
quins after all. Although it was a close call.

"You've been hungry ever since we arrived in
Bachelor Falls." Tori teasingly patted Ross's
belly and cut a conspiratorial smile to Ellie.
"You must have whetted his appetite with all
that popcorn you fed him his first night back."

Ellie lifted her chin and forced up the corners
of her lips in response. "It's just nerves," she
said and hated the possessive note she heard in
her own voice. "He'll be back to normal as soon
as the wedding's over."

Ross met her eyes and her heart broke for the
second time that day. He would be back to normal. And so would she. Just as soon as he married Tori and left Bachelor Falls for good.

"That's it. I'm only eating popcorn and sweets
and everything I can get my hands on because
I'm nervous." His eager tones made the statement an exaggeration and had everyone laughing
with him. It was only Ellie who didn't see the
humor.

"Oh, Ross, you bad boy." Tori rolled her eyes
at him. "Don't tell me you've been eating
sweets, too. You know that just destroys my image of you."

"You're right. Who needs sweets with you
around?" Ross kissed her cheek. The bridesmaids sighed. Reverend Minks looked on fondly.

The groomsmen blinked. Ellie looked closely to make sure it was Ross standing there and not Brad Elston with his glib romanticism. But it was Ross, so she calculated the time she'd need to bake chocolate chip cookies and a few more of Ross's favorite treats, and completely destroy his image before Saturday at six. But short of distributing the fat and calories in a reverse liposuction, there wasn't much she could do.

"Now, then..." Reverend Minks guided them gently back to the rehearsal at hand. "After the exchange of rings, Ross and Tori, I'll look over at Mrs. Perkins, like this—" he demonstrated the "look" "—and she will nod at Melva, who will stand and sing the selected hymn." He smiled patiently at the organist and the vocalist, who were practicing nodding and standing on cue. Melva Whiffington cleared her throat, but Reverend Minks was nobody's fool. "We won't take time to do the song now, Melva, thank you. I know you'll do a beautiful job at the ceremony. Now, once the song is through, I will put my hands over your clasped hands, Ross and Tori, like this—" He put their hands together and laid his palm on top. "Then I will say a few words. Then I'll smile, like this." He demonstrated the smile. "And then I'll say, 'Ross, you may kiss your bride.' And then, you'll kiss Tori, like—"

"This." Ross was nobody's fool, either, and he demonstrated the way he would kiss his bride.

And that, Ellie told herself on a wave of jealousy and regret, was the way this story was going to end.

"I'M NOT GOING." Ellie stood in the open vee of the El Camino's door and told Ross she was not going to the rehearsal dinner.

"You're going," he said, his expression stern and stubborn and settled. "It's my wedding. You're my best man. I need you with me at the rehearsal dinner."

"Oh, give me a break, Ross. You don't need me there. You'll have Tori and Chrissy and the other two attendants and—"

"They're nitwits."

"Your parents will be there. And her parents and—" She stopped to squint at him. "Did you just call Tori a nitwit?"

"No, just the gigglers from Chicago."

Ellie sighed and resumed the list of reasons he wouldn't miss her at the dinner. "Freda will be there. Reverend and Mrs. Minks."

"And Zombies I and II," he added, his lips curving at his perceptive description of Tori's cousins from Milwaukee.

But the smile wasn't real and it wasn't really for her. Ellie was beginning to think the smile she wanted to see again was gone forever. Stolen from her, along with so much more, in the kiss that hadn't happened.

"Eliot," he pleaded softly. "I want you there. Please."

"No, Ross. I've got a headache and—"

"Don't do that, Ellie." He put his hand on top of hers on top of the door and squeezed until it hurt. "Don't start making excuses. It's important to me for you to be at the dinner tonight. And if our *friendship* is important to you, you'll be there."

He might as well have slapped her. "What does that mean? You're going to start blackmailing me now? If I don't go to the rehearsal dinner, then I don't care about our friendship? What's next, Ross? If I don't want to go bowling with you sometime, does that mean our friendship isn't important to me? *Friends* don't put that kind of condition on things."

"Then maybe this isn't about friendship. Maybe this is about you and me."

Ellie stiffened and, for what seemed like forever, she stared into Ross's green eyes. Then, from some instinctive need to protect herself from hurt, she forced herself to relax, to pretend she didn't know what he was talking about. "I have a headache, Ross. I'm going home. And if you choose to let our friendship stand or fall on the truth of that, then maybe we don't really know each other anymore.''

ROSS WATCHED THE El Camino roll out of the church parking lot and would have given anything to go with it. But Tori was waiting for him. His parents, Freda, the Minks. They all expected him to be at the rehearsal dinner, expected him to be excited, happy, eager. Hell, he didn't even know all the emotions he was expected to have.

You're stressed. You're tired. You're getting married on Saturday. He tried the mantra that had gotten him through the past few days, but he didn't even know what it meant anymore. What he did know was that yesterday, before he and Ellie had kissed, he'd known his role, his place in the universe. And today he didn't.

''Ross?'' It was Tori, the woman that only yesterday he'd been certain he wanted to be with every day for the rest of his life. ''Let's go, sweetheart,'' she said with a smile. ''They're expecting us.''

With a reluctance that was becoming distressingly familiar, Ross turned toward her. *You're stressed. You're tired. You're getting married on Saturday.* Prewedding jitters, he told his heart firmly. Then he went to do what they all, even Ellie, expected him to do.

ON FRIDAY MORNING, Ellie parked the El Camino at the garage and walked the couple of blocks to Main Street. The Bachelor Daze festival was in full blossom, with vendors and booths striping the downtown area in vivid patterns and splashes of brilliant color. A dark green canopy stretched across the far end of the town square, where the barbecue lunch would be served from eleven-thirty to one o'clock. Barricades blocked off one corner of the Save-Rite parking lot, securing the area around a large stake-bed truck, known as the Freedom Trolley. After the race, the bachelors who weren't captured or otherwise thwarted in their attempt to run the gauntlet of determined women, would climb aboard the trolley and be transported to the falls for their official "dip."

The Bachelor Daze race rules forbade any female from stepping foot on the Save-Rite parking lot after two o'clock. The women grumbled that it handicapped their efforts to stop the bachelors from making it to the falls, but it saved Ernie Potts, who drove the Trolley, from accidentally running over any overzealous Bachelor Falls female.

As Ellie reached the center of town, a bus from Joplin was dropping off visitors in front of Taylor's Shoe Shop. John Webster, the chief of police, was directing pedestrian traffic with a whistle and his very own booming voice.

"Welcome to Bachelor Falls," he boomed. "The Bachelor Daze Race to the Falls starts at three o'clock right here on Main Street." The bus rumbled off to the designated tourist bus parking area by the post office and a fifteen-passenger van took its place in front of Taylor's. "Welcome to Bachelor Falls," Chief Webster's voice boomed again. "The Bachelor Daze Race to the Falls starts at three o'clock right here on Main Street."

Ellie made her way through the crowd, trying to see past the sightseers and discover whether Ross was waiting for her at their prearranged meeting place—in front of the bank's south doors. Her pulse raced at the thought of him and she made herself slow down, take the extra steps needed to stay calm, to arrive cool, collected and in control. She'd spent a long night thinking, arguing with her heart, remembering the kiss and telling herself to forget it. But she couldn't, and from that realization she'd formed a plan. Today was the last full day she might ever have to be with Ross and she'd decided to spend it doing her damnedest to convince him he wasn't in love with Tori.

"Ellie, hi!" Kelly called to her from across the street. "Cute outfit," she yelled, but the rest of her words bounced off the tops of about a million heads that bobbed between them. Ellie waved and moved on. Toward the place where Ross would be waiting.

Okay, so maybe she couldn't talk him out of getting married. Maybe it was wrong to even try. But she'd be doing him a favor. He'd thank her after this was all over. Just like all those other times when he'd been in love with the wrong woman, he'd come to his senses. He'd realize that she, his best friend in the world, had been right all along. He'd realize he was really in love with her. Ellie. That was the way this story should end.

"Eliot Applegate, I'll have a word with you, please." Like an avenging angel, Aunt Ona Mae appeared before her, blocking all avenues of escape with a stern look.

"I'm sort of in a hurry," Ellie began, only to be stonewalled by another sterner look.

"You are making a big mistake," Ona Mae said as if she knew.

Which she probably did. Moments like this, Ellie wondered if there really were Bostians out there in the cosmos, creating chaos, telling secrets. "Look, Aunt Ona Mae, I know what I'm doing. I thought about it all night and it's the right thing to do. The honest thing."

Ona Mae scooted the double straps of her

beige purse farther up her arm. "I wouldn't call it honest. I wouldn't call it honest at all."

Ellie's defenses rose. "Well, it is. It has to be. It's the only hope I have." She hadn't meant to say that. Hadn't meant to think it. But there it was. Her only hope was to convince Ross he was marrying a nitwit. And wrong or not, she was going to do it.

"Well…" Ona Mae stood there, arms crossed, back straight, purse dangling from her arm. "If your only hope for happiness is to dress up like a quarterback, then you need professional help." And with that and a nod of conviction, she walked straight as an arrow to the herbal booth. "Give me a package of that ginger root," she told the herbalist inside. "It's the only thing that stands between me and an alien abduction."

Ellie felt limp. And hot. The football uniform she'd borrowed as a joke was heavy and beneath the helmet, her hair felt gummy with perspiration. She'd thought the costume would make Ross laugh, would ease the tension between them, and pave the way for her to begin her seduction. Well, not seduction exactly, although that would be her fall-back strategy. If all else failed. If there was no other way to convince him he wasn't in love with Tori, that she was just the latest in a long line of nitwits.

"What are you doing in that outfit?" His voice came from behind her and she spun in all her Buccaneer finery to see Ross. Just looking at his familiar face made her breathless. Seeing his smile stopped the beating of her heart. And he was smiling. Her smile. The one she'd thought she might never see again. It was going to be all right, she thought. Because it had to be. It just had to be.

"I told you I had my padding ready. I'm here to escort you through the gauntlet, Ross. No one is going to stop you from making it to the falls on my watch."

"Speaking of watch, what time is it?"

"Don't know. Left my watch at home," she said with a saucy tilt of her head. "Didn't match my helmet."

He knocked on the red-and-gray helmet. "Lose the padding before you pass out from the heat and I have to carry you through the gauntlet. Then I'll never make it to the falls."

Relieved, Ellie removed the helmet and pushed her unruly hair out of her face, only to feel the damp tendrils come curling right back. "You'll make it," she said. "This is probably the only time in the history of the great Race to the Falls that a woman has had an excuse to make the run.

Believe me, nothing is going to keep us from getting through."

"Don't get cocky. I saw Tommie Nell with a basket of water balloons this big." He cupped his hands to indicate the size. "And you know Mabel and Hazel have been up all night getting the whipped cream pies ready. Are you *sure* you want to fight your way through that?"

"For you, Ross, I will brave anything. Even water balloons and whipped cream pies."

His smile turned melancholy. "I'm glad you're going with me this time, Eliot, even though I have no intention of actually jumping into the falls. I won't ever get to run the gauntlet again, you know."

"Cheer up," she said brightly. "You may get lucky and get pushed into the falls and have to stay single for another year."

"Mayor Jimmy's made a career out of it, hasn't he? Think Tommie Nell will ever get him to the altar?"

"My money's on her this year," Ellie said. "I think this will be his last run, too."

"I'm going to miss all this," Ross said, his attention sweeping the crowd and activity around them.

"You'll be back," she assured him. And herself.

"But it won't be the same. Nothing's going to be the same."

Standing there next to Ross, in the familiar, frenzied middle of the Bachelor Daze craze, she was careful not to touch him, careful not to let her love shine bright in her eyes, careful not to let him see that for her, nothing was ever going to be the same again.

Chapter Eleven

The starter's gun went off with a bang and the wall of bachelors jogged forward, cautious, watchful, knowing disaster could strike from anywhere along the cheering throng that lined Main Street. From the corner of her eye, Ellie saw Melva Whiffington dart out.

"On your right," Ellie yelled to Ross. "One o'clock!" He easily sidestepped Melva's advance, but got smacked with a water balloon when he got in between Tommie Nell and her target...Jimmy Bartlett. Ellie dodged a whipped cream pie that sailed over her head and caught Shorty Silvers on the arm. Laughing, she jogged on beside Ross. "This is fun," she said...just before Lana's mother jumped out and sprayed her with Silly String.

Ross grabbed her arm then and propelled her ahead of him, using her as a shield when Carla Ramsey aimed her Super-Dooper Water Gun at him. Ellie sputtered under the deluge and wished she hadn't given the football helmet to Chip, who was sprinting like a gazelle far ahead of the pack. Of course, no one really cared about the kids. It was only the really eligible men who made the race interesting.

"You're mine, Doc!" Belinda Morgan jumped out of a Porta-John and right in front of Ross. Before Ellie could tackle her, she had her arms around Ross's neck and was kissing him full on the mouth. There was no rule against kissing as a means of halting the men in their tracks, and there was no denying it was effective, but Ellie thought of it as taking unfair advantage. It seemed especially unfair when it was Belinda kissing Ross.

"Hey—" Ellie said as she grabbed Belinda's arm and tried to pull her off. But Belinda had suction and the will to succeed and Ross frankly wasn't putting up much of a struggle. In fact, his hands were suspiciously close to her—"Knock it off!" Ellie pinched him and Belinda at the same instant and then used her shoulder pads to bulldoze Ms. Morgan into the unsuspecting path of Brad Elston, who should have been paying attention instead of making eyes at the high school cheerleaders as they cheered and did high kicks in front of town hall.

"Brad!" Belinda beamed, and then pulled her

best strategy ever. Quick as a flash, she pulled up her T-shirt and flashed him.

Brad stumbled and went down for the count.

"Wow," Ross said, slowing in case Belinda tried a second flash.

"Keep running," Ellie advised. "And don't look back."

"It's a good thing you broke me out of that lip lock when you did," Ross said as they got blasted with another battery of water balloons. "She's a lot stronger than I remember."

"Yes," Ellie commiserated. "I noticed how hard you were struggling to break free."

He grinned, then winced as whipped cream splatted in great gobs across his cheek and ear. "No one ever said this was a picnic. The honorable estate of bachelorhood is at stake."

"So, you see this as a mission," Ellie said, tripping Stacy Halloran as the blonde tried to attach a clamp to Ross's trunks.

"Not a mission, exactly." He hopped forward, narrowly missing being snared by Hazel's expert toss of the fish net. "More like the quest for the Holy Grail."

Chrissy, apparently inspired by Belinda's tactical maneuvers, ran into Ross's path. But she was giggling so hard, Ellie was able to steer him clear of danger before Chrissy could get her lip lock set up.

"You were a little fast that time, Eliot," he said, ducking Mrs. Minks and her stun gun—a slingshot with bean bag ammunition.

"I'll keep that in mind." She pressed close to his side, steering him through an obstacle course of determined Bachelor Falls women.

"Hi, Ross!" Tori called meekly from the sidelines, her fingers curling down in a tiny little wave. Ross waved back, but the distraction cost him another delay. Tommie Nell, still chasing Mayor Jimmy, leaped over Henry Boyd, who was stooped down and frantically trying to work Thelma Perkins's lasso off his ankle. Tommie Nell plowed right into Ross, taking them both down.

She was up in a flash. "Out of my way!" she yelled. She chased off after Jimmy again, waving a pair of handcuffs. Ellie had just gotten Ross on his feet when a bouncy redhead on roller skates bumped him from behind, spun him around and jumped right into his arms. He looked a little surprised, but certainly not dismayed and Ellie began to see the gauntlet as not quite the hardship the men jokingly complained it was.

Stealthy movement caught her attention. "Watch out, Ross. Tami Ryals has you in her sights and... Man! Where did she get *that?*"

Ross dropped the redhead just in time to find himself staring down the nozzle of a homemade

water pistol—its design based loosely on a bag-
pipe, its size half again the circumference of a
watermelon. He just had time to reach for Ellie—who nimbly stepped aside before Tami
blasted away with what had to be six gallons of
green Jell-O. Fifteen seconds later, Ross had been
transformed into the Incredible "Jell-O" Hulk.
"Mmm," he said, licking his lips. "I always
have room for Jell-O."

Ellie laughed so hard her sides ached and she
almost missed seeing the female posse that was
moving in fast from the sidelines. "We'd better
get out of here."

"Oh, don't worry. It's going to take Tami a
little time to reload that pistol," he said, still
swiping slime off his face.

"Yes, but the cavalry is on its way in...and
Melva's in the lead."

"Hell," Ross said. "They're making a human
chain. We'll never get past them now."

"Psst! Kilgannon! Over here!" Help materi-
alized in the form of Travis and Bobby Joe, who
had opened a small avenue of escape in the jos-
tling crowd. They'd set up a kid's Slip 'N Slide,
all wet and waiting to provide a quick slide onto
the Save-Rite parking lot and into another year
of freedom.

Ross grabbed Ellie's hand and together, they

took a broad jump and slid the remaining length of Main Street.

THE FALLS AREA WAS PACKED with families, friends and shouts of laughter when the Freedom Trolley rumbled to a stop. Several of the younger bachelors, Chip and his cronies, leaped from the truck and raced ahead. By the time Ellie and Ross approached the official jump-off point, the natural pool at the base of the falls was dotted with males and a few more dived in every few minutes.

"Ross!" Chip shouted from the pool below. "Come on in! The water's great!"

"Colder than an ice-cold beer in December," muttered a dripping, shivering Shorty as he climbed up out of the water and grabbed a towel from the stack provided just for the occasion.

"Over here, Ellie. Ross." Reverend Minks was manning the temporary cleanup area. He had a bucket of water and a hose attached to the fire truck out in the parking area. His pant legs were rolled up, but he still had on his clerical collar and was all set up to wash off whipped cream, Jell-O or whatever other substances the bachelors had collected on their race to the falls. Fun was well and good, but the environment had to be protected and Reverend Minks was just the man for the job.

"Turn to your left," he instructed, and Ross obediently turned, letting himself be hosed clean. "Lift your right foot. Now your left. Now both feet at once. Ha, ha, just a little holy humor. Ellie, your turn."

She had already removed the football pads, but she hitched up the pants as she stepped up. Cold water from the hose poured across her legs and she shivered with the exhilarating tingle.

"Are you going to jump, Ellie?" Reverend Minks asked.

"She's got to make a stab at pushing me off, first." Ross stood nearby, bare-chested and wet from head to toe. Ellie was pretty sure if she got close enough to give him a push, she'd find herself trying to imitate Belinda and put a lip lock on him. "It's her duty as the best man to make an effort to get me in the falls and save me from impending matrimony."

"She may try," Reverend Minks said with his benign smile. "But I bet she won't succeed, will she? After all, it might be—" He leaned forward, lowering his voice to a teasing whisper. "—*bad luck* for you to get pushed into the falls on the day before your wedding."

"You don't put any faith in that legend, do you, Reverend?" Ellie asked, stamping her feet to get some circulation going. "I know you must have married at least a few bachelors who took a nosedive into the water on Falls Day and got married before the year was out.''

"One or two." Reverend Minks moved the hose back to the bucket and Ellie decided the cold was preferable to the heat she felt just looking at Ross in his swimming trunks. "I've always been of the opinion," the Reverend continued, "that those the Lord intends to be together, won't be kept apart by anything as unimportant as legends or bad luck or misunderstandings. He does have His mysterious ways, you know." He leaned close to whisper in her ear. "Give Ross a good, hard shove. Just between you, me and the Almighty, I think a dunking might clear his head." Smiling, he turned to the next survivor of the race. "Step right over here, young man...."

Ross grinned when Ellie came up beside him at the sign that read, Point Of No Return. Jump Or Get Yourself Hitched. "Guess it's you and me against the legend, Eliot."

"I thought it was me against you."

He raised an eyebrow. "Never that. No matter what, it'll always be us against them."

"It," she corrected. "The legend is an it."

"Hey, Kilgannon, save yourself, man! Jump!" From the viewing area on the other side of the falls, Travis, Tami, Carla and Bobby Joe were watching the jumps. The falls weren't high, but the pool was deep and the jump-off point was no higher than a regular diving board, which made for some spectacular belly flops.

Ross cupped his hands around his mouth and yelled across the whoops and hollers in the pool. "I'm not jumping. Ellie's going to have to push me...if she can."

"Go, Ellie!" The guys yelled and slugged the air with their fists.

"Don't do it, Ellie," Tami and Carla countered, laughing. "It's a trick!"

"Well, Eliot? What are you waiting for?" Ross held his arms out, giving her a solid expanse of lightly furred chest to push against. He stood there, grinning, waiting for her to make a move.

There was absolutely no truth to the legend. Ellie knew tomorrow's wedding wouldn't be called off because Ross went over the falls. On the other hand, if there was even a glimmer of truth to it... She took a step toward him and he feinted side to side, like a boxer in the ring, so she stopped. "Stand still," she said.

"Now, Eliot, that wouldn't be fair. Come on, you can take me. Have confidence. Repeat after me...*I think I can, I think I can.*"

"You're toast, Kilgannon. Prepare to die." She faked a lunge to the left, and quickly counter-pushed to the right, missing him by a mile.

"Go, Ellie!" Tami yelled out. "Grab that boy and get him away from the water!"

"Push him!" Bobby Joe hollered. "Send him flying over the edge!"

Travis sang out, "Missed him, missed him, now you've gotta kiss him!"

Ross's grin grew by leaps and bounds. "Think you can get a lip lock on me before I get past you?"

"That would be cheating." She lunged, her palms making contact with his chest. But he was ready for her and easily held his ground. Beneath her hands, she felt the rapid thud of his heartbeat and she felt her own heart pounding, hard and fast. Her eyes lifted to his and, for a moment, she wondered what would happen if she did try the lip lock. The idea zipped through her veins with more zest than she needed to acknowledge. Dropping her hands to her sides, she stepped back to consider her strategy.

"Giving up, already?" he taunted. "You didn't put up much of a fight, Ellie. You must want to be my best man very badly."

She wasn't a man, damn it, and maybe it was time she used that fact to her advantage. Reaching for the hem of the football jersey, Ellie jerked it upward, faking a Belinda-style *flash*.

"Ellie!" Ross protested and grabbed for the shirt.

And that's when she rushed him, putting all her weight behind the push of her outstretched hands.

It was a moment that would live forever in the annals of Bachelor Falls history. The moment Ross Kilgannon went over the falls...and took his best man with him.

Chapter Twelve

Ellie turned, checking her image in the mirror for probably the hundredth time in twenty minutes. She seldom wore a dress, and when she did, she had to keep checking to make sure it wasn't hitched up in the wrong places, that it still draped where it was supposed to drape and covered where it was supposed to cover. Not that this dress had much drape...or coverage. It curved where she curved, and flared where she flared and showed a lot more of her than normally showed. When she'd bought it, Kelly had assured her it was as flattering as hell. Which was the reason it had been hanging in the back of her closet ever since.

Ellie sighed. Maybe she wasn't cut out for seduction. And seduction was what all her plans had fizzled down to. There hadn't been five minutes during the day to talk seriously to Ross about Tori. There hadn't been a minute when the opportunity and the mood meshed. And there had been several times when she wondered if she had any right to say anything at all. Ross had driven Hot Rod in the morning parade, all shiny and gleaming in her new candy apple red coat. Tori had been beside him, waving like a queen to her subjects...and Ellie had stood by and watched the Chevy...and Ross...pass her by. It had been all she could do not to rush out, snatch the keys from the ignition and order Tori out of *her* car. But it wasn't hers. She'd given it to Ross. And she was glad...she'd just wanted to be the one riding in it with him.

And tonight she was going to tell him that. She was going to be honest and open about her feelings and try to convince him that she wasn't the best man, but the woman he wanted. Or at least the one he ought to want. That's where the little black dress was supposed to come in. Sort of warn him right at the start that something was different about her.

But what if he didn't notice?

Ellie turned for another check. The dress still clung smoothly to her hips, still felt ridiculously insubstantial. Which was good, she thought. She'd be so busy checking her butt in every shop window, she wouldn't have time to wonder if she was doing the right thing.

''He doesn't want to marry Tori,'' she assured

her reflection. "He doesn't." But the only way she knew to convince him of that was to startle him out of his infatuation. There wasn't time for anything more circumspect. This time tomorrow, it would be too late. So this was the bargain. She'd pit her hope of happiness against the idea that he was already falling out of love. She would wager their friendship against his infatuation and pray that, if she were wrong, he would forgive her. Someday.

With one last glance at her backside, she gathered her courage and headed for town.

HIS JAW DROPPED when he saw her.

Ross had just ordered a lemonade when he looked up and realized the sleek, sexy body in the little black dress, the body he'd been admiring in brief glimpses across the town square, belonged to Ellie. He'd always known she had a nice figure, but he had had no idea she could look like *that*.

"Ross?" From inside the refreshment booth, Mabel handed him a lemonade. "You better drink that quick. You look like you just got whopped with a water balloon. 'Cept, of course, you ain't wet."

Ross grabbed the glass from her hand and drank the lemonade in one long swallow. Damn, he thought. What in hell was *Ellie* doing in that dress?

"You must be thirsty," Mabel said, taking the glass back. "I'll fix you another lemonade."

Ross didn't want another lemonade. He didn't want to be standing by the lemonade booth, watching an Ellie he barely recognized come toward him. She walked differently in a dress, he thought inanely. The dress was certainly formfitting. And she certainly had a form worth fitting. And she had no business moving her hips like that. The Bachelor Daze Dance was, after all, a family event. Ross tried to force his gaze away from that seductive walk as she came closer.

Unfortunately he couldn't seem to tear his eyes from her. Only the fact that she stopped to talk to Lana and her new husband, Blake, saved Ross from making a complete fool of himself by ripping a tablecloth off the nearest table and draping it around her.

Fifties' music was blasting over the loudspeakers and several couples were dancing in the street to a rowdy version of "Rock Around the Clock." Ross felt out of place, out of time. Ellie was throwing him curves, faster than he could catch them. One minute she was the same old Ellie, laughing, teasing, fun. The next minute she was someone else altogether. Someone he didn't know at all, except by heart.

He gulped when she turned in his direction again. Her hair was long, loose, not confined in any way…a direct contrast to the way the little black dress fit her. No, he wasn't going to think about the way she looked in that dress. Or the way she walked. Or the way her hair… No, no, no. This was Ellie. His friend. But the closer she got, the more he thought about the dress…the walk…the hair….

"Hi," she said brightly. Too brightly. "Where's Tori?"

Ross noticed the slight wince, as if she hadn't wanted to mention Tori at all. "The bridesmaids took her over to Branson to see a show. It's her official bachelorette party."

Ellie nodded, looked nervous. He wondered if he looked nervous, too. "The last time I saw you in a dress, Eliot, you were on your way to seduce some unsuspecting fraternity man." His knees went a little weak at the memory and he told himself that seduction could not be what she had in mind tonight. Not that it was any of his business, of course.

She stepped closer, right up to the counter, right next to him…and his throat went unaccountably dry. He tried not to notice the full curve of her breasts just below the dress's neckline. He especially tried not to observe the beautiful line of her back as she leaned in, looking for someone to fill her drink request. "Didn't I see Mabel here just a second ago?"

"Yes." One syllable squeaked into two and Ross made a conscious effort to lower his voice. "She should be back any minute now."

Ellie frowned up at him, her wild mane of hair draping like silk across one shoulder. "You're not catching a cold, are you? Your voice sounds kind of thick."

"Allergies," he said promptly, making a production of clearing his throat before he repeated the explanation. "Allergies."

"Oh." Then she turned her head and her hair showered down across her back and his throat went dry all over again. "Mabel?" she called. "Could I have something to drink?"

Mabel hustled back. "Sure can. This is for Ross, but I'll be back with one for you in just a sec."

Ellie cleared her throat, as if huskiness was contagious. "Do you have any wine?"

Wine? Ross wondered. "I didn't know you liked wine."

Sexy was all over the slight curve of her mouth and layered like cream through the smoky nuances of her voice. "Maybe you don't know me as well as you think you do, Dr. Kilgannon."

He was damn near certain of it. "Maybe you

ought to just tell me what you're trying to pull, Eliot, so I can tell you what a bad idea it is.''

She blushed, took the wineglass Mabel handed to her, and downed two ounces of Merlot in one gulp. ''What makes you think I'm up to something?''

He crossed his arms over his navy Polo shirt. ''For one thing, slamming back shots of Merlot can only mean you're drinking for courage, not pleasure.'' She looked at the empty wineglass, obviously unable to refute that particular bit of evidence. ''And for another thing, you don't dress like this unless you have an agenda.''

She glanced down at the dress, and looked guilty. But when she raised her chin and her coffee brown eyes met his, he decided the look might not have been guilt at all. He was imagining all sorts of things at this very minute and the guilt might very well be all on his end.

''So if I dress up and drink wine, then it logically follows that I have an agenda that's a bad idea? *Hmm.*'' She considered that with a tilt of her head. ''When Tori puts on a dress and drinks wine, does *she* have an agenda?''

''No. Yes. We're not talking about Tori.''

''Well, maybe it's time we—'' A glimmer of panic flashed across her expression. ''—had another drink. Mabel? Hit me again!''

Mabel narrowed her eyes. ''Now what are you

up to, Ellie? I ain't never seen you drink wine before.''

Ross appreciated the support of his theory. Ellie apparently didn't.

"I'm thirsty. Okay?" She stubbornly held out the empty glass and Mabel just as stubbornly refused to fill it.

"Then I'll get you some lemonade," the older woman said and went off to do so.

Ross tried not to look at her with an I-told-you-so expression, but she didn't even glance at him. Just crossed her arms under the bustline of the little black dress and leaned back against the booth beside him. "If you were any kind of a gentleman, Ross, you'd get me a glass of wine."

"If I were any kind of a friend, I'd take you home before you do something you'll regret later."

She gave him a hesitant little half smile. "How do you know I'd regret it?"

"I'm just going on past experience, Ellie. You've got that look."

"The look that says if I don't do this, I'm going to regret it for the rest of my life?" Her voice was so still, he had to lean forward to catch her words. "Or is it the look that says, if I do this, at least I'll have done one thing in my life worthy of regret?"

The night breeze lifted a strand of her hair and

blew it soft against his mouth and when she turned her face toward him, he lost his heart. All of it. In an instant. In that one look. In that one wistful, regretful, hopeful look, he suddenly understood all the ambivalence of the past few days. All the stress, all the tension, all the reasons he'd wanted to be with Ellie and not his soon-to-be bride. He was in love with Ellie. He must have always been. *T. S. Eliot Kilgannon has a nice ring to it,* he'd said only a few days before. No wonder it had sounded so natural and right. He wanted to share his name with her, just as he'd shared everything else these past many years.

Mabel came back with the lemonade. He took it right out of her hand and chugged it down, excitement and panic and desire urging him to take action, to stop and think, to ask Ellie if maybe she loved him, too. He slapped the empty glass on the counter again. "Bring us two glasses of wine, Mabel," he said fast, then reconsidered. "Hell, just bring the whole bottle."

Mabel looked at him as if he'd suddenly declared war on Nova Scotia. "What?" he said defensively. "I'm thirsty."

Ellie's glance was startled, but wary. "Did you have a sudden change of agenda, Ross?"

Plans were forming like summer showers in his brain. He considered and discarded them like a musician seeking the right sequence of notes. "I want to dance. Let's go."

"I thought you wanted wine. I thought you were thirsty."

"We'll come back for it," he said. "Right now we're going to dance."

Ellie hesitated. "You want to dance with *me?*"

"Yes," he answered as firmly as possible over the terrible, thudding beat of his heart. "Yes. You."

"Oh," she said, and he reached for her hand before she could refuse.

Ellie's fingers trembled against his palm and it was all he could do not to kiss her then and there. A real kiss. Not an accident in the dark. But a kiss they could build a future on. A kiss worthy of their long friendship. A kiss that would mark the moment they crossed over from that friendship to so much more. A kiss he didn't want to share with half the population of Bachelor Falls.

"Where are we going?" Ellie asked, her voice sounding still and uncertain and wary. Very wary. "The street dance is happening over there."

"We don't want to dance."

"We don't? I thought we did."

"You thought wrong." He shook his head and

changed direction when he saw Brad Elston and Belinda Morgan in their path.

"Ross," Belinda said, "Brad and I want to—"

Ross stepped up the pace and pulled Ellie into an abrupt right turn, avoiding whatever it was Belinda and Brad wanted.

"She could have had something important to say," Ellie pointed out.

"She didn't." Ross realized they were only a block away from the garage and the length of his stride increased eagerly. Ellie broke into a semi-jog to keep up and he automatically slowed down. "Sorry," he said. "Guess I'm in something of a hurry."

"You're heading in the wrong direction again."

He smiled and kept walking. "This is the first time I've been heading in the *right* direction for years."

The lights and noise of the town square faded and Ellie's heels made a sharp clicking duet, accompanied by the steadier thudding of his cordovan loafers. He held her hand tightly and he meant to never let go.

"This is the way to the garage."

"So it is," he replied. "I want to check on Hot Rod."

"It's Rodette, now, remember?"

The garage came into view, a sprawling, bulky shadow, as familiar as the street beneath their feet and the stars above their heads. He was walking so rapidly he was very nearly pulling her with him as he passed the office and approached the back garage bay where he'd left the Chevy after the Bachelor Daze parade.

"I'm sure the Chevy is fine, Ross." Ellie sounded confused and wary. Still wary. But not for long, he thought. Please, God, not for long.

"There's just something I have to do here." Taking the key from his pocket, he unlocked the door, stepped inside and pulled her in behind him.

She found the light switch first and flipped it on. "See?" she said, looking at the Chevy. "She's right here where you left her."

"Yes." Emotion roughened his voice as he put his hands on Ellie's shoulders and turned her to face him. "Right here. So close, I nearly missed seeing her at all."

Her eyes met his, there in the garage bay where they'd laughed and talked and worked and played, where they'd grown out of childhood and into love. "Ross?" She whispered his name as a question.

But he was pretty sure she knew the answer even before he bent his head and claimed the kiss that turned the whole world right side up.

Chapter Thirteen

Ellie hadn't had many dreams come true, but she had no trouble recognizing that this—the dream she had barely allowed herself to dream—was the only one that mattered.

"Ross," she whispered when she could breathe again. "Ross, I don't know what to... say. I didn't know.... I never imagined this.... I—"

"Love you," he supplied before she could. "I love you. I mean, I *really* love you." Wonder was in his eyes as he cupped her face in his hands. "I must have loved you since the moment you first propositioned me."

Somewhere, she thought, there was a rainbow. No, not somewhere. Here. In Ross's arms. "I've never propositioned you."

"You did. In fifth grade. It was my first real proposition."

"Sixth grade," she corrected. "And it wasn't a real one."

"You asked me to be your bodyguard. I consider that a real proposition. And from now on, I'm taking the assignment very seriously."

"Mmm." She pressed her lips to the slight indentation beneath his chin and then worked her way up to his mouth...because the taste of intimacy was so new, so very intoxicating. Some moments later, she whispered, "I don't need a bodyguard."

"Doesn't matter. You've got one." He curled his fingers into her hair. "For the rest of your life or mine, Eliot, I'm guarding your body. And your heart. And your health. And your wealth. And anything else that crops up between now and then. But this will be a reciprocal arrangement."

Ellie's heart beat so hard, she thought he surely must hear it. "Ross," she whispered. "I never knew I could feel like this...until the other night, in my tent. Before that, I never really thought you and I..."

Tenderly he looped her hair behind her ear. "Never is behind us, Ellie. Forever begins right here, right now."

A tear slipped from the corner of her eye, followed by another and another. Silent. Sweet. The way tears ought to be. "I love you," she whispered and wondered how three simple words could ever convey the complexity of the feeling inside her. "I love you."

He caught one of the teardrops on his fingertip and pressed it to his lips. "I think this is the first time I've ever seen you cry," he said. "Except for that time when you got so mad about the tree house."

"The time my best friend decided to convert our tree house into a *boys only* club?"

"We ended up including you," he reminded her.

"Only because I was the one with the ladder."

"No, because we were all afraid of you."

She tilted her head back to look up at him, thinking that this was what it felt like to have everything. "When did you stop being afraid, Ross?"

"About fifteen minutes ago by the lemonade booth, when you looked up at me and I knew I was in love for the first and the last time in my life." He kissed her then, and passion flared like rockets and shooting stars and everything bright she could imagine. This was real. This was happening. This was the moment she had never had the courage to hope for. The moment that suddenly, miraculously, was hers.

She threaded her fingers through his hair, wondering at its rich, silky texture, marveling that she was free now to touch it with the hands of a lover. Incredibly, he gathered her closer...until there wasn't a sliver of air between the intimate melding of their bodies, until the very breath she took was somehow his, until their hearts beat in a lovely, lusty harmony. Ross was everything dear and familiar to her and yet, his touch was all uncharted, strange and new. How could she have known him forever and not known his kiss would be so intensely gentle, so hot, so tender, so meltingly possessive?

But in a million years she could never have guessed the way his mouth would feel against hers. She could not have imagined any emotion to equal the thrill of being held fast in his arms. How could she have conceived of any feeling that would have been even remotely comparable to the excitement coursing through her at this very instant? And there was no way on earth or in heaven that she could ever have pictured herself as dizzily happy as she was right now.

Ross, her favorite companion, her childhood protector, her dearest and best friend, was now her lover, her heart...her life.

"Ross," she whispered.

"Ellie," he whispered back.

And all the other words she wanted to, needed to, thought she must say, bloomed still and silent and reverent there in the garage. Or maybe it was simply that the words traveled an unfamiliar, but well-worn path straight from her heart to his.

"WHAT WOULD you think about taking Hot Rod for a spin?" he asked sometime later. "I think it's time the two of us went cruising in *our* classic Chevy."

Ellie didn't want to say what had to be said, but she lifted her chin and tried not to lose her courage in the face of his incredible tenderness. "I think it's time we talked about…tomorrow."

"Tomorrow," he repeated as if he couldn't remember the significance. But then he nodded and she knew he was as reluctant as she to face the unpleasant task that stood between them and the forever they'd just begun. "Tomorrow's the wedding," he said. "I guess I should let Tori know it isn't going to happen."

"She deserves that, Ross. And I deserve to know that you're not imagining yourself in love with me in order to escape from this commitment you've made to her."

His hand stroked her cheek, her neck, her hair, as if he could never get enough of touching her. "This isn't about escape, Ellie. It's about truth. Until a little while ago, I didn't know that my truth was you. I thought it was in doing what everyone expected me to do. Becoming a surgeon, living in Chicago, marrying a cute little blonde and having three children. I knew it didn't feel exactly right, but…'' He shrugged. ''I want to be here, Ellie. With you. And that's the truth. None of the rest of it matters.''

Ellie closed her eyes for a second, savoring the words and the shower of sweet possibilities that now stretched like a bed of roses before her. But she'd been practical all her life. And falling in love hadn't changed that. ''It matters until you've talked to Tori,'' she said. ''It matters a lot.''

''Then I'll find her now.'' His finger traced the slope of her nose, the trembling line of her mouth, the faint quiver in her chin and the look in his eyes swept away the last trace of doubt. ''I'll find her and explain that I can't marry her…because I've fallen in love with my best man.''

Ellie laughed or cried. It was hard to tell amidst the jumble of emotions inside her heart. ''I love you, Ross,'' she whispered softly. ''Find her…and come back to me.''

His lips clung to hers for a moment out of time and place and then he stepped back and tapped the end of her nose. ''If that's a proposition, Eliot, I accept.''

THE CHURCH WAS BATHED in summer watermelon pink and spring showers green. Bachelor Falls residents were wearing their Sunday best and their Saturday smiles. Already, at only a quarter past five o'clock, the pews were filling fast. Thelma Perkins was already ten minutes into her repertoire of wedding songs and Melva Whiffington was in the choir room, exercising her voice. Reverend Minks had been in and out of his office so many times during the past hour, Ellie was losing count. "Any word from Ross?" he'd asked brightly each time...as if he was positive there was nothing to worry about, even though he obviously was worried.

Truth to tell, Ellie was worried herself. She hadn't seen Ross since he'd left her at the garage and gone to look for Tori. He'd called a few times—well, several times actually—just to hear her voice, just to tell her he would rather be with her than driving to Branson to find his erstwhile bride. But the last call had been at two o'clock and he had yet to get to talk to Tori.

Ellie battled a sudden, horrible fear that he had run away, that he wasn't going to cancel the wedding, that he was halfway to Nashville. Or Alaska. But that type of thinking wouldn't solve anything, so Ellie didn't allow herself to think it at all. Ross was doing what he had to do in order to come to her, free of any other commitment. Their friendship, their love, deserved nothing less.

So, not knowing what else to do, she'd come

to the church, wearing her rented tux. And here she'd been waiting for the past hour, checking her watch from time to time as the art deco hands moved inexorably toward the wedding hour with no sign of the groom.

Reverend Minks smiled as he entered the office again. "Ross is here," he said in a tone that implied he hadn't been worried for a minute. "He just drove into the parking lot. So if you fellas—" the reverend indicated Ellie and the personality twins with a nod "—want to get the getaway car all decorated and tied with cans, you might want to slip on out there and get started."

Tori's cousins nodded and left, presumably to find tin cans. Reverend Minks waited with Ellie, who couldn't sit, couldn't stand, couldn't be still. The moment Ross opened the door and walked in, though, she couldn't do anything except stare at him. He looked tired, unhappy and panicked. At least, he did until he saw her and then his smile lit up the world. "Hi," he said and walked over to take her hands in his. "How are you doing?"

"Hi," she replied softly. "Did you find her?"

He shook his head. "I drove to Branson as soon as I left you last night, but couldn't find her anywhere. I must have cruised the parking lots of a hundred motels looking for the car. And then I tried phoning around, trying to locate her. Finally I drove home, thinking I could catch her here, but those nitwits she calls her friends are bound and determined to stop me from seeing or even talking to her before the wedding. It's bad luck, they tell me. Even my mother won't take a note to her." He squeezed Ellie's fingers so hard, it hurt. But the physical discomfort felt good. Took her mind off the mounting apprehension in her heart. Canceling the wedding was one thing, waiting until the last hour to do it was another. "I'll find her," Ellie said. "She'll talk to me. I'll tell her it's an emergency and that she has to see you before the wedding."

Ross gathered her into his arms and kissed her thoroughly, passionately, completely. "I should have thought of that myself. I love you, T. S. Eliot Applegate. With all my heart."

Reverend Minks coughed into his fist, reminding them of his presence in the room. "I see a slight, uh, problem has arisen."

Ross kept hold of Ellie's hands. "I'm not going to marry Tori, Reverend Minks. I can't. It would be a mistake because—" his gaze came back to Ellie "—because I realized—"

"You realized you're in love with your friend Ellie." Reverend Minks nodded as if he'd known it all along. "That's wonderful." His round face was suddenly creased with a frown. "Wonderful, but bad timing. Very bad timing."

"I know," Ross said. "I've made an honest effort to find Tori and tell her, but now…"

"I'll find her," Ellie said, reaching for the door. "Where are the bride and bridesmaids getting dressed, Reverend?"

"In the prayer room," he replied. "But Tori isn't with them. She's around here somewhere, because I saw her once but now no one knows where she went."

Ross took a deep breath. "Okay, then. I'm going out there and tell everyone that the wedding is off. This has to stop before Tori actually starts down the aisle. I never meant to hurt her and I certainly don't want her to suffer any more embarrassment than…"

There was the briefest of knocks on the door before it opened and Tori came in. The flounces of her bridal gown took over the room, as fluffy and fussy as a gown made out of cotton candy. "Ross?" she whispered. "I have to talk to you."

Reverend Minks nodded and skirted the flounces to reach the door. "I'll be outside if you need me," he said. "Just tap on the door like this…." He demonstrated a soft one-two rap. "And I'll come back in…if you need me, that is."

Ellie freed her fingers from Ross's hand and took a step after Reverend Minks, but Tori stopped her. "Don't go," she said. "Maybe this will be easier if you're here."

Someone had gotten to Tori first, Ellie thought. She knew about Ellie. She knew...and that made Ellie feel tawdry and cheap.

"I've been trying to talk to you since midnight," Ross said, his voice low and steady, but threaded with determination. "No one would let me near you."

"I know." Tori twisted something in her hands. Something that crackled. "I asked them to do it, Ross. I'm sorry, but I just couldn't face you. I thought if I got ready for the wedding— as if it was actually going to happen—then everything would turn out all right and we'd be so happily married that I'd never even think about..." The crackle came and went beneath her nervous hands.

Ellie felt awful. For Tori. For Ross. For herself. Maybe this moment had to happen. Maybe it was kinder to hurt Tori in this way than in the more public arena of the church sanctuary. But it didn't seem kinder to Ellie. It seemed awful. Simply awful.

"Tori—" Ross began.

"I won't do it, Ross, if you tell me it's foolish beyond anything. But this could be my chance to be famous, to be *Tori!* I know there's a lot of things that could go wrong, but I have to try. You understand, don't you?''

''What are you talking about?'' Ross's concern became flat-out confusion. ''What did you say about your chance to be famous?''

Her blue eyes widened. ''You don't know? Chrissy didn't tell you?''

''What was Chrissy supposed to tell me?''

''Oh, she wasn't *supposed* to tell you. But I figured she would. She can never keep a secret. I didn't want her to, of course. I thought it was only fair that I be the one to tell you, even though I didn't want to. And really, Ross, if you say I should forget it, I will. I'll marry you and forget all about my dream of becoming the next Reba McEntire. I will. But this promoter heard me sing last night at the karaoke bar in Branson and he came up afterward and talked to me about coming to Nashville and making a demo. And...'' She paused to draw a deep, trembly breath. ''Oh, Ross, I really want to go.''

Ellie brushed her fingers against Ross's, communicating with him in a touch that everything was going to be okay. ''You don't want to marry me?'' Ross asked, surprise and a note of self-directed humor building in his voice. ''You came here to say you're calling off the wedding?''

Tori nodded and smoothed out the crumpled cellophane in her hand. A Twinkies wrapper, Ellie noted, and felt better all around. Maybe Ross and Tori hadn't been such a mismatch after all. Not that they'd ever know for sure. Not that it mattered anymore. Not that anything mattered except that Tori was jilting Ross. Right here. Right now.

"But if you still want to get married," Tori continued. "I'll call Earl…he's the producer and…"

"Are you sure he's on the level, Tori?" Ross asked. "I mean, there are some guys who might say they represent a recording studio when in actual fact, they're just—"

"Sleazebags." Tori nodded. "I checked him out, believe me. That's where I've been almost all day. Talking with an entertainment attorney, going over the contract with a fine-tooth comb." She smiled. "I'm not a complete nitwit, you know."

"I never for a moment thought you were." Behind his back, Ross found Ellie's hand and squeezed it.

"I'll stay, though, if you want, Ross." Tori clearly wanted to have it all. The recording contract *and* the brokenhearted, jilted groom she left behind. It was the stuff country songs were made of. "I'll give up my dream if you say the word."

Ross cleared his throat. "No, Tori. That wouldn't be fair. Not to either one of us. If you don't take this opportunity, you'll always regret it. Oh, maybe not today. Maybe not tomorrow. But someday. And for the rest of your life. And I..." He sighed dramatically. "I couldn't live with that regret. So, go. Go and be the star you always dreamed of becoming. And one day I'll be able to say..."

He paused and Tori rushed in. "You'll be able to say, you forgive me," she concluded with a dramatic little sigh.

"I'll be able to say I knew you when..." He smiled as she rushed forward and planted a fleeting kiss on his lips.

"You're wonderful, Ross Kilgannon." She breathed out the words in tightly held excitement. "Isn't he, Ellie? Isn't he absolutely the most wonderful man you've ever met?"

Ross looked at Ellie expectantly and she shrugged. "He has his moments. He writes some pretty great song lyrics, too."

For the first time, Tori looked at Ross with genuine interest. "You never told me that, Ross."

He shrugged. "The moment never seemed right."

"Well, don't think I'll forget you when I'm a star. Because I won't. I'll send you free tickets to my concerts and everything." She giggled with the sheer thrill of her imagination. "So, I'm off,'' she said and giggled some more. ''Wish me luck!'' Tori turned for the door, her flounces bouncing around her. ''Oh. You will tell my folks, won't you, Ross? Tell them I'll call them from Nashville. Tell them I'm going to be a star!''

Then the door was opening and she was flouncing through and Reverend Minks was leaning in to check for problems. ''Anything I can do?'' he asked kindly.

''Yes,'' Ross gathered Ellie's hands in his. ''Tell everyone that there isn't going to be a wedding. Not today. Tell them the gifts will be returned and that everything will work out just fine. Tell them the bride's happy. Tell them the groom's happy. And...''

''Tell them the best man is *very* happy.'' Ellie laid her head against his shoulder and smiled at Reverend Minks. ''Be sure to tell them that, too.''

Reverend Minks nodded, his round face beaming with a smile. ''So the story ends like this, huh?''

Ross summed up. ''The wedding's off. The bride is off to Nashville to become a singing star. The groom is off to...'' He smiled at Ellie. ''Ever been to Las Vegas?''

''Never,'' Ellie answered, smiling at him with all the love, all the memories, all the hope her heart could hold. "I've heard weddings there are something out of this world."

"The Bostians have relocated there." Ross gave her a wink, then started for the door. "So, that's the story, Reverend," he said. "No wedding today. Just three complete happily ever afters."

"Bachelor Falls will never settle for that, Ross," Ellie reminded him. "We'll have to tell them every detail of how it all happened."

"We will," he agreed. "At our wedding reception. Right after we get back from Vegas. Tell them that, too, will you, Reverend?"

"Be happy to. Anything else?"

Ellie laughed. "Tell everyone Ross has eloped with his best man."

Then Ross pulled her through the door and toward a future that sparkled as shiny and bright as Hot Rod's new paint.

The spring 1998 forecast calls for...

April 1998: **HERE COMES THE...BABY**
Pam McCutcheon
A front of morning sickness sets in with
temperatures rising at the onset of a sexy secret
dad. Highs: Too hot!

May 1998: **A BACHELOR FALLS**
Karen Toller Whittenburg
Heavy gusts of romance continue as a warming
trend turns friends to lovers just in time for one
friend's wedding...to someone else!

June 1998: **BRIDE TO BE...OR NOT
TO BE?** Debbi Rawlins
Expect a heat wave as the handsome hunk
building a bride's dream house sends soaring
temperatures through her fantasies.

Available wherever Harlequin books are sold.

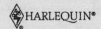

Take 4 bestselling love stories FREE

Plus get a FREE surprise gift!

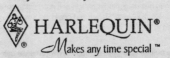

MEN at WORK
All work and no play? Not these men!

April 1998

KNIGHT SPARKS by Mary Lynn Baxter

Sexy lawman Rance Knight made a career of arresting the bad guys. Somehow, though, he thought policewoman Carly Mitchum was framed. Once they'd uncovered the truth, could Rance let Carly go...or would he make a citizen's arrest?

May 1998

HOODWINKED by Diana Palmer

CEO Jake Edwards donned coveralls and went undercover as a mechanic to find the saboteur in his company. Nothing— or no one—would distract him, not even beautiful secretary Maureen Harris. Jake had to catch the thief—*and* the woman who'd stolen his heart!

June 1998

DEFYING GRAVITY by Rachel Lee

Tim O'Shaughnessy and his business partner, Liz Pennington, had always been close—but never *this* close. As the danger of their assignment escalated, so did their passion. When the job was over, could they ever go back to business as usual?

MEN AT WORK™

Available at your favorite retail outlet!

Looking For More Romance?

Visit Romance.net

Check in daily for these and other exciting features:

Hot off the press

View all current titles, and purchase them on-line.

What do the stars have in store for you?

Horoscope

Hot deals

Exclusive offers available only at Romance.net

Plus, don't miss our interactive quizzes, contests and bonus gifts.

PWEB

HARLEQUIN®

AMERICAN ◆ ROMANCE®

COMING NEXT MONTH

#729 WANTED: DADDY by Mollie Molay
Jeremy and Tim knew exactly what kind of father they wanted, but
nothing they did made their mom go out and find him. The boys had no
choice: they had to take matters into their own hands and kidnap a dad!

#730 THE BRIDE TO BE...OR NOT TO BE? by Debbi Rawlins
Showers

Kelly was looking forward to her button-down small-town life with ol'
reliable Gary in their soon-to-be-built new home. So why, then, was the
sexy carpenter igniting her with his searing glances that threatened to
burn down her white picket defenses?

#731 HUSBAND 101 by Jo Leigh
Shy Sara Cabot was assured *Thirty Steps to Sure Success with the Opposite
Sex* would work for anyone. Then she tried them on a hunky ex-navy
SEAL. The steps were guaranteed...but to do what?

#732 FATHER FIGURE by Leandra Logan
Charles Fraser was used to doing his father's bidding, so how bad could
becoming a father figure to his five-year-old nephew really be? But then
he met the boy and his hard-to-resist mom....

AVAILABLE THIS MONTH:

#725 DIAGNOSIS: DADDY
Jule McBride

#727 A BACHELOR FALLS
Karen Toller Whittenburg

#726 A COWBOY AT HEART
Judy Christenberry

#728 A LITTLE BIT PREGNANT
Charlotte Maclay

Look us up on-line at: http://www.romance.net